Fragments of Reality

Zephyr Wrenwood

Published by Solstice Skylancer, 2023.

While every precaution has been taken in the preparation of this book, the publisher assumes no responsibility for errors or omissions, or for damages resulting from the use of the information contained herein.

FRAGMENTS OF REALITY

First edition. October 1, 2023.

ISBN: 979-8223821007

Written by Zephyr Wrenwood.

Table of Contents

Chapter 1: Whispers Between Worlds 1

Chapter 2: Echoes of Atlantis...4

Chapter 3: The Heart's Song..6

Chapter 4: Fragments of Unity...9

Chapter 5: Whispers in the Depths......................................13

Chapter 6: Unraveling Secrets 18

Chapter 7: The Heart's Descent 22

Chapter 8: Shadows and Sunlight.......................................26

Chapter 9: Whispers in the Dark...30

Chapter 10: A Glimpse of Truth...34

Chapter 11: On Pillars of Hope and Despair......................37

Chapter 12: Whispers in the Wind......................................40

Chapter 13: Echoes of the Past..43

Chapter 14: A Glimmer in the Gloom 47

Chapter 15: Fragments of the Past.......................................50

Chapter 16: Unraveling Threads 55

Chapter 17: Echoes of the Past..59

Chapter 18: Unveiled Truths 64

Chapter 19: Echoes of Time 68

Chapter 20: The Heart's Veil...72

Chapter 21: Fractured Realms and Unseen Hands.............77

Chapter 22: A Dance with Shadows 81

Chapter 23: Reunion and Revelations.................................85

Chapter 24: Fragments and Friendships.............................88

Chapter 25: Echoes of the Past..91

Chapter 26: The Core's Secrets..95

Chapter 27: The Place Between Dreams 99

Chapter 1: Whispers Between Worlds

The early morning sun cast a soft golden glow over the town, bathing the streets and houses in its warm embrace. Alice, her short, wavy brown hair bouncing with every step, hurried down the cobblestone path, her backpack filled with books, a peculiar electronic device, and a sandwich her mother had packed for lunch.

She reached the gates of her school, a grand old building with a large clock tower that always seemed to chime a minute too early. It wasn't the lessons or the teachers that made her rush; it was the anticipation of accessing the new history simulation the school had installed.

"Beat you again!" exclaimed Kai, her tall and lanky friend, as he skidded to a stop beside her. His cheeks were flushed, and his dark eyes twinkled with mischief.

"You had a head start!" Alice retorted, but her teasing smile gave away her lack of genuine indignation.

Zara, with her tightly coiled hair and freckled face, joined them moments later. "Honestly, you two and your races," she said with a playful roll of her eyes. "What's the rush? We have all day to explore the simulation."

Before either could respond, the school bell rang, its echo reverberating through the still morning air. The three friends exchanged a quick glance, knowing their moment was close.

Mrs. Halley, their history teacher, was already at the front of the classroom when they entered. A kind-faced woman in her mid-forties, she wore her silver hair in a neat bun and had a penchant for floral dresses.

"Good morning, class," she greeted, her voice soft yet firm. "Today, we'll be diving into the lost city of Atlantis. Please make your way to the simulation room."

A ripple of excitement washed over the students. The simulation room was the crown jewel of the school. The walls were lined with holographic projectors, and in the center stood a large platform upon which the simulations would be projected.

Alice, Kai, and Zara took their places side by side. As the lights dimmed, the room transformed, transporting them into the world of Atlantis. Vibrant coral reefs surrounded them, and fantastical sea creatures darted through the waters. Majestic, shimmering buildings of gold and silver towered overhead, their spires reaching for the surface.

"Remember," Mrs. Halley's voice echoed around them, "this is a learning experience. You may look, but do not interact."

But as Alice gazed at the ethereal beauty of the Atlantean city, a peculiar sensation washed over her. She felt a strange pull, a magnetic connection to this world. Turning her gaze, she saw a glowing pattern on the palm of her hand, one she had never noticed before.

"Do you see that?" she whispered to Zara and Kai, showing them her hand.

Kai squinted, but Zara's eyes widened. "I've read about this," she whispered. "It's said that certain individuals have a deeper connection to historical events. Maybe you..."

But before Zara could finish her sentence, a group of Atlanteans approached. Their faces, a blend of curiosity and concern, were focused squarely on Alice's glowing hand.

The trio exchanged a worried glance. They were just visitors, observers of history. But somehow, in this moment, history itself seemed to be reaching out, intertwining with their very existence.

And Alice, with the glow of Atlantis reflecting in her eyes and the weight of a mysterious connection pressing on her heart, knew that her journey was only just beginning.

Chapter 2: Echoes of Atlantis

The Atlanteans, draped in shimmering robes that reflected the myriad hues of the ocean, approached the trio with a mixture of fascination and caution. Their leader, a statuesque woman with flowing aquamarine hair, stepped forward, her gaze fixed intently on Alice's glowing palm.

"Who are you, young traveler?" she inquired, her voice a melodious song that seemed to ebb and flow with the rhythm of the surrounding waters.

"We... We're students," Alice stammered, trying to recall Mrs. Halley's lessons on Atlantean etiquette. "We come in peace, just to learn."

The Atlantean woman studied Alice for a few seconds before nodding slowly. "You bear the Mark of the Ancients," she said, pointing to Alice's hand. "A symbol of connection and understanding between worlds. I am Lysandra, the High Priestess of Atlantis."

Zara, her wide eyes revealing her astonishment, leaned towards Alice. "I've read about her," she whispered, "but I thought she was just a myth."

Lysandra smiled warmly. "There are many myths about our city, young one. But as you can see, some have roots in reality."

Kai, not one to be easily daunted, piped up, "Why can we interact with you? Aren't we just observing?"

Lysandra looked thoughtful. "The Mark," she began, "it blurs the lines between observer and participant. It's rare, but in times of great need, someone bearing the Mark can cross the boundaries and connect with our world."

Alice, her curiosity piqued, looked at her hand. "But what does it mean? Why do I have this?"

Lysandra's eyes held a touch of sadness. "The Mark chooses its bearer for reasons not always clear to us. But its appearance now suggests that Atlantis faces a challenge that requires an outsider's perspective."

Just then, a loud clang echoed through the city, causing the water around them to ripple and shudder. Lysandra's face grew tense. "That's the second time this week. Our city's protective barriers are weakening."

Zara looked concerned. "Barriers?"

Lysandra nodded. "Mystical shields that protect our city from outside threats and maintain its balance. But recently, they've started to falter."

Alice felt a weight in her chest. "Is there anything we can do to help?"

Lysandra looked at Alice with a glimmer of hope. "Perhaps. But first, you must learn about the heart of Atlantis, the source of our city's power."

The trio exchanged glances, the weight of their unexpected responsibility settling upon them. They were no longer mere observers; they had become participants in a narrative that could shape the fate of Atlantis.

As Lysandra led them deeper into the city, past magnificent buildings and bustling marketplaces, Alice couldn't shake off the feeling that their unexpected adventure was only just beginning.

Chapter 3: The Heart's Song

The deeper they ventured into Atlantis, the more Alice felt the weight of the city's ancient history. Grand statues lined the boulevards, telling tales of brave Atlantean heroes and the challenges they had faced. Fountains with sparkling water danced under the ever-shifting light, and above them, the city's ethereal dome shimmered, a testament to the magic that held the ocean at bay.

Lysandra led them to a building that stood apart from the rest, its architecture a blend of elegant simplicity and grandeur. "This is the Temple of Memories," she said, her voice echoing slightly in the vast entranceway.

Inside, the temple was even more breathtaking. Walls of luminescent coral glowed softly, their lights reflecting off the water's surface and creating intricate patterns on the ceiling. In the center of the room stood a pedestal, upon which rested a radiant crystal. Its pulsating light seemed to breathe life into the room, casting vibrant hues in every direction.

"That," Lysandra whispered with reverence, "is the Heart of Atlantis."

Kai, ever the curious one, asked, "Is it some kind of power source?"

Lysandra nodded. "Yes, but it is more than just that. The Heart not only powers our city but also stores our collective memories, hopes, and dreams. It is the embodiment of our past and the beacon for our future."

Zara looked at the Heart with wonder. "It's beautiful," she murmured.

Alice, feeling the pull of the Mark on her palm, stepped closer. "How is it that the barriers are failing if the Heart still shines so brightly?"

Lysandra sighed deeply. "The Heart draws its strength from the unity and shared purpose of our people. Lately, there's been discord. Doubts have crept in, causing fractures in our unity. The Heart senses this dissonance, and its power wanes."

Alice hesitated before asking, "And you believe I can help?"

The High Priestess met her gaze, her blue eyes searching Alice's. "The Mark you bear is not just a symbol of connection but also of healing. We believe that with your unique perspective, you might find a way to mend the rifts that have formed among us."

Kai looked skeptical. "But we're just kids. What can we possibly do?"

Lysandra smiled gently. "Sometimes, it is through the innocence and simplicity of a child's view that the most profound solutions are found."

Suddenly, the temple was filled with a hauntingly beautiful melody. Voices joined in harmony, singing of hope, unity, and a brighter future. Alice felt the song resonate deep within her, its melody intertwining with the rhythm of her own heart.

"These are the Voices of Atlantis," Lysandra explained. "Ordinary citizens who come to the temple to share their hopes and dreams, adding them to the collective consciousness stored within the Heart."

Alice felt a tug on her arm. Zara, her eyes bright with excitement, whispered, "Do you think we could join them? Share our own hopes and dreams?"

Lysandra overheard and nodded encouragingly. "It is an ancient tradition, but perhaps, in your voices, the Heart might find the harmony it seeks."

With a mixture of trepidation and excitement, the trio joined the circle of singers. Taking a deep breath, Alice closed her eyes and let her voice flow, her song a blend of her own hopes and the memories she had formed with Kai and Zara.

As their voices rose in harmony, the Heart of Atlantis pulsed brighter, its radiant light filling the temple, casting away shadows, and for a brief moment, bridging the worlds of Atlantis and the visitors who had come to help.

When the song ended, the room was silent but for the gentle hum of the Heart, its light now steady and strong.

Lysandra approached the trio, her face alight with hope. "Perhaps," she murmured, "there is a way to heal our city after all."

And Alice, with the weight of a city's hopes resting on her young shoulders, knew that their adventure in Atlantis was far from over.

Chapter 4: Fragments of Unity

The morning after their enchanting performance at the Temple of Memories, Alice, Kai, and Zara were woken up by the soft, harmonious chimes of Atlantean bells. They had been offered accommodations within the temple, and as Alice opened her eyes, the serene glow of the coral walls welcomed her to a new day.

Stretching and looking around, Alice noticed Kai and Zara, still half-asleep, tangled up in their blankets, the aquatic textures of the sheets shimmering in the room's gentle luminescence. She smiled, her heart warm with the thought of how their bond had grown over this unexpected journey.

However, thoughts of their mission soon took over, and the weight of their responsibility pressed upon her. The city's unity was fragile, and they had to find a way to help the Atlanteans mend the fractures that were weakening the Heart.

After a breakfast of exotic fruits and what seemed to be Atlantean versions of pancakes, the trio were joined by Lysandra. She had arranged a tour of the city, hoping it would offer insights into the discord that had seeped into the community.

Their first stop was a bustling marketplace, where Atlanteans traded everything from shimmering fabrics to mysterious artifacts. Kai's eyes widened in awe as he noticed a stall with intricate gadgets, devices that merged ancient designs with a touch of otherworldly technology.

"Can we take a look?" he asked eagerly.

Lysandra nodded, a hint of amusement in her eyes. "Of course. Understanding our way of life is crucial to your task."

As Kai rushed over, Alice and Zara wandered to a nearby stall where a craftsman was sculpting delicate figures from a radiant material that seemed half-liquid, half-solid. As he worked, he hummed an old Atlantean tune, his fingers moving in harmony with the melody.

"These are beautiful," Zara whispered, her fingers grazing a figure of two intertwined dolphins.

The craftsman looked up, smiling warmly. "Thank you, young traveler. These sculptures are crafted with memories, each resonating with an emotion or a moment in time."

Alice tilted her head, intrigued. "Crafted with memories?"

He nodded. "Yes. In Atlantis, art and memories are deeply entwined. We believe that by capturing memories within our crafts, we can relive those moments and share them with others."

Listening intently, Alice felt the stirrings of an idea. What if the key to restoring unity lay in the city's art? In sharing and understanding each other's memories?

Lysandra, noticing Alice's contemplative expression, gently inquired, "What's on your mind?"

Alice hesitated for a moment, gathering her thoughts. "The craftsman said art and memories are intertwined here. Perhaps the way to heal the rifts is to encourage Atlanteans to share their memories, their dreams, their fears, and find common ground through art."

Lysandra looked thoughtful. "That's an insightful observation. The recent discord has created barriers between citizens, causing them to withdraw and keep their memories to themselves. By sharing them, we might indeed rediscover our shared identity."

As they continued their tour, the trio sought opportunities to understand the city's soul. They visited schools, where young Atlanteans were taught the importance of unity and harmony; they observed communal rituals at sacred sites, where citizens joined in song and dance; and they spent time at recreational zones, where Atlanteans of all ages engaged in games and friendly competitions.

Throughout the day, they noticed subtle signs of the discord Lysandra had spoken about. Arguments erupted over trivial matters, and there seemed to be an underlying tension in the air.

That evening, as they gathered in the temple's main hall, Alice shared her observations and the idea that had taken root in her mind.

"We need to host a grand festival," she began, "where everyone in Atlantis can come and share their art, their memories, and their dreams. A celebration of unity."

Zara's eyes sparkled with excitement. "And we can have different zones! One for music, one for crafts, one for storytelling!"

Kai added, "And maybe some for tech and inventions. The gadgets I saw in the marketplace were amazing!"

Lysandra, listening intently, nodded. "It's an ambitious idea, but it might be exactly what we need. Atlantis has not seen such a festival in centuries."

The next few days were a whirlwind of activity. The trio, along with Lysandra and a team of volunteers, worked tirelessly to organize the festival. Invitations were sent out, stages were set up, and artists from all corners of the city were encouraged to participate.

The day of the festival dawned bright and clear. The city was abuzz with excitement, and as the first rays of light filtered through the dome, the Heart of Atlantis pulsed with a renewed vigor.

The festival was a resounding success. Atlanteans came together, sharing their art, their memories, and their dreams. The air was filled with laughter, music, and the sounds of joyous celebration.

Alice, watching from a balcony, felt a warmth spread through her. This city, with its ancient magic and modern challenges, had found a way to come together, to find unity in diversity.

As the festival drew to a close, Lysandra approached the trio, gratitude shining in her eyes. "You have done more for Atlantis than you can imagine. The Heart is stronger, and the barriers are healing."

Alice smiled, holding up her hand, the Mark glowing softly. "We just helped you find the way. The real strength lies within Atlantis and its people."

The journey in Atlantis had been an unforgettable one, filled with wonder, challenges, and the timeless lesson that unity could heal even the deepest rifts.

Chapter 5: Whispers in the Depths

Following the grand festival, the mood in Atlantis was jubilant. Alice, Kai, and Zara could sense the change everywhere they went: in the cheerful greetings of passersby, the spontaneous melodies hummed by groups of children, and the vibrant artwork that now adorned the walls of every building.

One morning, as the trio sat by the city's luminous central fountain, sipping on a sweet Atlantean beverage, Zara posed a question. "Have you ever wondered why the Heart of Atlantis was vulnerable in the first place? I mean, it's an ancient artifact, right? There must be a deeper reason for the fracture."

Kai nodded, swirling his drink thoughtfully. "It's been bothering me too. Lysandra said that the discord among the people was affecting the Heart, but isn't that kind of... backwards? Shouldn't the Heart, being so powerful, influence the people instead?"

Alice, ever the introspective one, leaned back, looking up at the translucent dome overhead. "I've been thinking about that too. It's almost as if there's a piece of the puzzle we're missing."

Their musings were interrupted by Lysandra, who approached them with a hurried step. Her face was drawn, and she looked more serious than they had ever seen her.

"Good morning," she greeted, her voice carrying a note of urgency. "I hope I'm not interrupting. There's something we need to discuss."

The trio exchanged glances. "What's wrong?" Alice asked.

Lysandra motioned for them to follow her. Leading them through winding alleyways and down a series of ornate staircases, she finally brought them to a secluded alcove, its walls adorned with intricate, ancient carvings.

"I've brought you here because it's one of the few places in Atlantis where conversations can remain private," she began, her voice low. "Something's happened."

Zara frowned. "What do you mean?"

Lysandra took a deep breath. "Late last night, one of our sentinels reported seeing a shadowy figure near the Heart's chamber. When they approached, the figure vanished. But this morning... the Heart's pulse is weaker."

Kai's eyes widened in alarm. "You mean someone's tampering with the Heart?"

Lysandra nodded. "We can't be certain, but it's a possibility we can't ignore. And that's not all. Whispers have begun to spread – rumors of a group, a faction within Atlantis that wants the Heart's power for themselves."

Alice's mind raced. "But the festival, the unity... Was it all just a distraction?"

Lysandra shook her head. "No, the festival was real, and its effects genuine. But there's always been a minority, a group who believes the Heart's power should be harnessed for personal gain."

Zara clenched her fists. "We can't let that happen. We've seen how beautiful and harmonious Atlantis can be."

Lysandra sighed. "Unfortunately, it's not that simple. This group, if they truly exist, are masters of deception. And they've always remained in the shadows."

Alice looked around, her gaze settling on the ancient carvings. "There's so much history here. Have they always been a part of Atlantis?"

Lysandra nodded slowly. "Legends speak of a faction, long ago, that sought to control the Heart. They were stopped, but it seems their ambition never truly died."

Kai scratched his head. "So, what do we do? How do we find them?"

Lysandra's eyes gleamed with determination. "We must be vigilant. Observe, listen, and gather information. This faction is clever, but they're not infallible."

Over the next few days, the trio, with Lysandra's guidance, set out to uncover the mysterious group's identity and intentions. They attended gatherings, visited marketplaces, and spent hours at the city's libraries, pouring over ancient texts.

One evening, as they sat in a quiet corner of the library, Zara stumbled upon a passage that made her heart race.

"Listen to this," she whispered, beckoning the others. "'When the shadows rise and the Heart falters, seek the Keeper of Echoes. Only they hold the key to unmasking the darkness.'"

Alice looked intrigued. "The Keeper of Echoes? Who's that?"

Kai frowned, thinking hard. "I remember hearing a story about a being, someone who can communicate with the past, with memories long forgotten. Could that be the Keeper?"

Lysandra looked thoughtful. "It's possible. The Keeper of Echoes is a title passed down through generations. They serve as the guardian of Atlantis' history, ensuring our memories are never lost."

Zara's eyes sparkled with excitement. "Then we need to find the Keeper! They might have the answers we're looking for."

The group agreed, and the next day, guided by Lysandra's knowledge and the city's oldest residents' stories, they embarked on a journey to the Keeper's sanctuary, located in the city's deepest depths.

Navigating a labyrinth of corridors, they finally arrived at a chamber unlike any they had seen before. The walls pulsed with light, and a series of crystal pillars stood in the center, each emitting a soft hum.

A figure, draped in flowing robes, emerged from the shadows. Their face was ageless, their eyes a deep shade of blue, reflecting the vastness of the ocean.

"Welcome," the Keeper intoned, their voice echoing softly. "I have been expecting you."

Alice stepped forward, the Mark on her hand glowing brightly. "We seek your guidance, Keeper. There are shadows in Atlantis, and we need to uncover the truth."

The Keeper nodded slowly. "The past holds many secrets, and the echoes of memories can guide you."

As they spoke, the chamber's crystals began to glow even brighter, illuminating a series of images: ancient ceremonies, battles, and celebrations.

"These are the memories of Atlantis," the Keeper explained. "And within them lies the key to unmasking the faction that seeks the Heart's power."

The group watched in awe as the memories played out, searching for clues. Hours seemed to pass in the blink of an eye.

Finally, the Keeper spoke again. "There is one memory, long buried, that may hold the answer. But be warned, it is a memory steeped in darkness."

The atmosphere in the chamber grew tense as a new image formed: A group of cloaked figures, their faces obscured, gathered around the Heart of Atlantis. As they chanted, the Heart's glow dimmed, and shadows crept in.

Alice gasped. "That's them! The faction!"

The Keeper nodded. "Yes. And if you look closely, you'll see that one of them bears a mark."

As they squinted, trying to discern the details, Kai suddenly pointed. "There! On their hand. It's... it's the same as Alice's!"

Alice looked down in shock, her own Mark glowing in response. "But... how?"

The Keeper's voice grew grave. "It seems the ties that bind you to Atlantis run deeper than any of us realized."

Before they could process this revelation, the chamber's entrance burst open, and a group of armed guards stormed in. At their head was a figure they all recognized: Lysandra.

Her face was a mask of betrayal. "You shouldn't have come here," she hissed.

Chapter 6: Unraveling Secrets

The atmosphere in the chamber was thick with tension. Alice, Kai, Zara, and the Keeper stared at Lysandra and the guards, unsure of what to expect. The beautiful, caring mentor they had come to trust now seemed like a stranger.

"Why, Lysandra?" Zara whispered, her voice quaking with disbelief. "Why would you betray us?"

Lysandra's face twisted into an odd smile. "Betray? Oh, sweet Zara, it's not betrayal if I'm merely ensuring the safety and future of Atlantis."

Kai stepped forward, his jaw set in anger. "By leading a faction that wants to control the Heart for themselves? That's your idea of 'ensuring safety'?"

Lysandra sighed, shaking her head. "You just don't understand. The Heart's power, if harnessed correctly, could do wonders. We could rebuild Atlantis to its former glory and beyond."

Alice's mark pulsed brightly, drawing Lysandra's gaze. "And me?" Alice asked, her voice surprisingly steady. "How do I fit into your plans?"

Lysandra's eyes glittered with a mix of pity and greed. "Ah, dear Alice. The last of the line with the Mark. You're the key to everything. With you, we can access the full power of the Heart."

The Keeper, silent until now, finally spoke. Their voice resonated with deep wisdom. "Lysandra, what you seek is not balance but dominance. Power without responsibility is a dangerous game."

Lysandra chuckled. "And you, old Keeper, think your ancient echoes can stop me?"

The Keeper tilted their head slightly, their ageless eyes meeting Lysandra's fiery ones. "Echoes of the past are not merely memories; they are lessons. Have you not learned from our history?"

Lysandra sneered, her patience wearing thin. "Enough of this! Guards, seize them."

As the guards moved in, Kai quickly whispered, "Stay close." He had a plan, but it required timing.

Zara, eyes darting around, spotted a cluster of crystals nearby. Recalling the lessons from the Atlantean books, she murmured a quick incantation. The crystals started glowing brilliantly, creating a blinding light that temporarily stunned Lysandra and her guards.

Taking advantage of the momentary confusion, Kai led the group toward a concealed passage he'd noticed earlier. "Hurry!"

They raced through the narrow corridor, with the sounds of the pursuing guards echoing behind them.

Emerging into a large cavern, they found themselves surrounded by an iridescent lagoon. The water shimmered with colors, reflecting the various minerals embedded in the cavern walls.

Zara's eyes widened in realization. "The Lagoon of Reflections! Legends say its waters can show visions of truth and reveal concealed intentions."

Alice approached the water's edge, feeling an inexplicable pull. As she gazed into the depths, images started forming:

She saw a younger Lysandra, fiercely training in secret, her face marked by determination. A series of events followed: secret meetings, the formation of the faction, and the slow infiltration of their ideas into Atlantis' governance.

But there was another vision, one that surprised them all. It showed Lysandra, tears streaming down her face, as she held a tiny baby. The child bore a mark, strikingly similar to Alice's.

Lysandra's voice whispered, "My darling, they won't understand. But one day, they will see the power you possess."

Alice reeled back, the weight of the revelation heavy on her chest. "She... she's my mother."

Kai and Zara exchanged stunned looks. The Keeper, however, nodded slowly. "The echoes never lie. They reveal truths, sometimes uncomfortable, but always necessary."

Zara gently took Alice's hand. "Alice, I know this is a lot to take in. But we need to keep moving. Lysandra's guards will be here soon."

They quickly made their way out of the cavern and into a dense underwater forest. The forest was a maze of glowing seaweed and coral structures, offering perfect cover.

As they navigated the tricky terrain, the weight of the revelation weighed on Alice. "Why didn't she tell me? Why keep it a secret?"

Kai placed a comforting arm around her. "People often have reasons for the things they do, Alice. Reasons that might not make sense to others."

Zara chimed in, "We'll figure this out, Alice. Together."

The Keeper, guiding them expertly through the forest, added, "Fate works in mysterious ways. Perhaps this revelation is the key to restoring balance in Atlantis."

Emerging from the forest, they found themselves at the edge of a cliff overlooking a vast abyss.

"The Abyss of Despair," the Keeper said solemnly. "Many have tried to cross it, but few have succeeded."

Alice took a deep breath. "We have to try. We can't let Lysandra control the Heart."

Kai nodded. "Together, we can do it."

Drawing upon their bond and the knowledge they'd acquired, they started their treacherous journey across the abyss.

However, as they were halfway across, a shadow loomed above them. Lysandra, flanked by her guards, had caught up.

"This ends now!" she shouted, her voice echoing menacingly

.But before anyone could react, the ground trembled, and the abyss began to collapse. Everyone started falling, plunging into the dark unknown.

Chapter 7: The Heart's Descent

The feeling of free-fall was jarring, the world around them a blur of darkness and echoes. Alice's heart raced, a knot of fear tightening in her chest. Her hand instinctively reached out, finding Kai's. Their fingers intertwined, providing a sliver of comfort in the midst of chaos.

Zara, with a determined look, conjured a shimmering protective sphere around them, slowing their descent. The Keeper, hovering beside them, radiated a calming energy, their presence always a source of stability.

As the group continued to descend, the darkness around them began to shift, revealing swirling patterns of light and color. The abyss, rather than being a void of nothingness, was alive with memories and emotions.

"What is this place?" Alice whispered, her voice trembling with a mix of awe and trepidation.

The Keeper responded, "This is the repository of Atlantis's collective memories, its soul. The Abyss of Despair is not just a physical descent but a journey into the heart of our civilization."

Kai, ever the protector, tightened his grip on Alice's hand. "So, these lights and colors... they're memories?"

The Keeper nodded. "Yes. And if one knows how to navigate them, they can provide guidance and answers."

Zara looked around, her eyes reflecting the myriad colors. "It's beautiful. But how do we navigate this? We can't stay here forever."

Before the Keeper could answer, a particularly vivid memory caught Alice's attention. It was of a young woman, bearing a striking resemblance to Lysandra, playing with a toddler. The child laughed gleefully, her innocent eyes reflecting pure joy. Alice's heart ached. "That's... that's me, isn't it?"

The Keeper nodded gravely. "Yes, Alice. Your memories, as well as Lysandra's, are a part of this tapestry."

Tears welled up in Alice's eyes. "But why? Why did she leave me? Why all this secrecy and betrayal?"

Kai gently squeezed her hand. "Maybe the answers are here, Alice. We just have to find them."

Alice nodded, taking a deep breath. "Let's keep going."

As the group delved deeper, they encountered more memories: moments of joy, sorrow, love, betrayal, and hope. Atlantis's history unraveled before them, showcasing its rich tapestry of emotions and events.

Suddenly, a memory caught Zara's attention. It was of a young Keeper, being chosen and trained. Their journey from an ordinary citizen to a guardian of Atlantis's wisdom and knowledge. "Is... is that you?" Zara asked the current Keeper.

The Keeper smiled, a hint of nostalgia in their eyes. "Yes. That was a long time ago. But my journey, like everyone's here, is a part of this abyss."

Kai, ever curious, posed a question. "If this abyss contains all of Atlantis's memories, does it also hold the key to controlling the Heart?"

The Keeper's face became somber. "Perhaps. But be wary, young Kai. Not all memories are meant to be revisited. Some hold power, both good and bad."

Just then, the group was jolted by a sudden force, pulling them towards a particularly dark cluster of memories. They struggled, trying to resist the pull, but it was too strong.

As they were drawn closer, Alice could make out the scenes: a great battle, Atlantis in ruins, the Heart being used as a weapon, and Lysandra, looking much younger, at the center of it all.

Zara, panic evident in her voice, shouted, "We need to get away from this! It's too powerful!"

But it was too late. The memory engulfed them, pulling them into its dark embrace.

When the darkness receded, they found themselves in the middle of the great battle. Chaos reigned, with Atlanteans fighting each other, the city in flames. Lysandra, wielding the Heart's power, stood atop a dais, her voice commanding and powerful.

Alice, though horrified, felt a strange connection to this memory. She approached Lysandra, her steps hesitant. "Why? Why are you doing this?"

Lysandra's gaze met hers, filled with pain and determination. "To save Atlantis, my dear. To save you."

The memory shifted, and the group was back in the abyss, the weight of what they'd witnessed heavy on their hearts.

The Keeper spoke, their voice filled with sorrow. "That was a turning point for Atlantis. And for Lysandra. It was the day she decided to take matters into her own hands, no matter the cost."

Kai, his face pale, whispered, "We need to find a way out of here. Before it's too late."

But before they could make a move, another force began pulling them, this time towards a brilliant, radiant light. The group, unable to resist, was drawn towards it.

As they approached, they realized it was not a memory, but a

portal. Beyond it, lay another world, its beauty and serenity in stark contrast to the chaos of the abyss.

Zara, her face reflecting hope, spoke up. "Could this be the way out? The key to controlling the Heart and saving Atlantis?"

The Keeper nodded, a hint of optimism in their eyes. "Perhaps. But be careful. For every light, there's a shadow."

The group hesitated for a moment, then, hand in hand, stepped through the portal.

But as they did, a chilling voice echoed through the abyss, stopping them in their tracks.

"Alice," it hissed. "You cannot escape your destiny."

Chapter 8: Shadows and Sunlight

The transition from the abyss to this new world was almost seamless. One moment, Alice, Kai, Zara, and the Keeper were surrounded by the swirling memories of Atlantis, and the next, they stood in a vast meadow, bathed in sunlight. The scent of blooming flowers, the gentle chirp of birds, and the warmth of the sun on their skin was a stark contrast to the chilling darkness they had just left behind.

Zara blinked, her eyes adjusting to the light. "Where are we?"

The Keeper gazed around, absorbing the beauty. "It's the Nexus of Dreams, a realm between realms. It's said to be the heart of all creation."

Kai squinted, shielding his eyes with his hand. "It's beautiful, but also... overwhelming."

Alice felt a flutter in her chest. The Nexus was familiar, yet strange. It felt like a place she had visited in a distant dream, but the details were just out of reach. "This place... it's like something out of a storybook."

Suddenly, a soft voice echoed through the meadow, melodious and kind. "That's because it is, dear Alice."

The group turned to see a woman standing a few feet away. She was of average height, with flowing silver hair that reached her waist. Her eyes, a brilliant shade of emerald, sparkled with wisdom and warmth. Dressed in a flowing white gown, she seemed to radiate an ethereal glow.

"Who are you?" Zara asked, her tone cautious.

The woman smiled, her eyes twinkling. "I am Elara, the Guardian of the Nexus."

The Keeper stepped forward, bowing slightly. "It's an honor to meet you, Guardian Elara."

Elara nodded in acknowledgment. "And it's a pleasure to welcome you to the Nexus. But tell me, what brings you here?"

Alice hesitated for a moment, then replied, "We're searching for a way to control the Heart and save Atlantis."

Elara's expression became somber. "Ah, the Heart of Atlantis. A powerful artifact, indeed. But with great power comes great responsibility."

Kai frowned, puzzled. "But how do we control it? How do we harness its power for good?"

Elara beckoned for them to follow her. As they walked through the meadow, she explained, "The Heart of Atlantis is not just a physical artifact. It's a manifestation of the collective soul of Atlantis. To control it, one must understand and connect with that soul."

Zara, always the pragmatic one, interjected, "That sounds poetic, but how do we actually do that?"

Elara chuckled. "By understanding yourselves. The Heart reflects the innermost desires and fears of its wielder. To control it, you must first control yourselves."

The group exchanged glances, processing Elara's words. It was Alice who spoke next, her voice filled with determination. "We're ready to do whatever it takes."

Elara smiled, her gaze lingering on Alice. "I know you are, dear. But be warned, the journey ahead is fraught with challenges."

As they continued walking, the meadow gave way to a dense forest. The trees were tall and majestic, their leaves a brilliant shade of gold. It was in this forest that the group encountered their first challenge.

Out of nowhere, a shadowy figure appeared, blocking their path. It was a creature, half-human, half-beast, with piercing red eyes and sharp claws. It growled, its gaze fixed on Alice.

Alice stepped back, fear evident in her eyes. "What is that?"

Elara's face darkened. "It's a Shade, a manifestation of your deepest fears."

Kai stepped forward, ready to defend Alice. "How do we fight it?"

Elara replied, "You don't. You face it."

Alice took a deep breath, summoning her courage. She stepped forward, meeting the Shade's gaze. "I'm not afraid of you."

The Shade hesitated for a moment, then lunged at Alice. But instead of attacking, it dissolved into a cloud of smoke, disappearing into the forest.

Elara nodded in approval. "Well done, Alice. By facing your fears, you've conquered them."

The group continued their journey, encountering more Shades along the way. With each challenge, they grew stronger, learning to face their fears and insecurities.

Finally, after what felt like hours, they reached a clearing in the forest. In the center stood a majestic tree, its trunk adorned with intricate carvings. At its base was a small, shimmering pool of water.

Elara gestured towards the pool. "This is the Mirror of Truth. It reflects the true nature of those who gaze into it. To control the Heart, you must first confront your true selves."

One by one, the group approached the Mirror. Each saw a reflection of themselves, but with subtle differences. Some saw versions of themselves that were kinder, others saw versions that were more confident or brave.

When it was Alice's turn, she hesitated. But with a gentle nudge from Elara, she stepped forward and looked into the Mirror.

What she saw took her breath away. Her reflection was not of her current self, but of a younger Alice, innocent and carefree. The young Alice smiled, reaching out a hand towards her older self.

Tears filled Alice's eyes. "I miss her," she whispered.

Elara placed a comforting hand on Alice's shoulder. "We all have parts of ourselves that we miss. But they're still a part of us, always."

Suddenly, the clearing was plunged into darkness. The group looked around, panic evident on their faces. From the shadows emerged a familiar, chilling voice.

"You may have conquered your fears," it hissed, "but you cannot escape your destiny."

And with that, the shadowy figure lunged at Alice, dragging her into the darkness.

Chapter 9: Whispers in the Dark

The forest, once alive with the gentle hum of nature, fell eerily silent. The golden leaves of the majestic trees stood still, as if time itself had paused. Zara, Kai, and the Keeper, their faces pale with shock, stood rooted to the spot where Alice had been taken. The darkness that had swallowed her seemed impenetrable, a void from which there might be no return.

Kai was the first to find his voice, his tone tinged with desperation. "We have to find her. We can't let her be taken by that... that... thing!"

Zara nodded, her eyes scanning the surrounding shadows. "But how? Where did it take her?"

The Keeper, usually so composed, looked deeply troubled. "The shadow is a manifestation of the Nexus's darker side. It thrives on fear and doubt. Alice must be somewhere within its realm."

Suddenly, Elara stepped forward, her emerald eyes shimmering with determination. "Fear not. The shadow cannot keep Alice for long. With your combined strengths, you can bring her back."

Kai, his face a mask of worry, asked, "But how? What do we need to do?"

Elara pointed to the Mirror of Truth. "The mirror can guide you. But remember, the path you take will be treacherous. You will face tests that will challenge the very core of your being."

The Keeper stepped forward, his gaze fixed on the mirror. "We're ready. We have to be, for Alice's sake."

Elara nodded. "Very well. Each of you, look into the mirror. It will show you the way."

One by one, Zara, Kai, and the Keeper approached the Mirror of Truth. As they gazed into its shimmering surface, the world around them began to blur and shift. The golden forest faded, replaced by a landscape of shadows and whispers.

The trio found themselves in a vast, desolate plain. The ground beneath their feet was cracked and dry, and the sky above was a deep, inky black. The only source of light came from a distant, solitary lantern, its glow casting long, dancing shadows.

Zara shivered, pulling her cloak tighter around her. "This place... it feels so... cold."

Kai nodded, his eyes scanning the horizon. "We need to find Alice. Let's head towards that lantern."

As they made their way towards the distant light, the whispers grew louder. Ethereal voices echoed all around them, their words a mix of warnings, regrets, and unfulfilled desires.

"Turn back... It's too late... You'll never find her..."

Kai clenched his fists, trying to block out the voices. "We have to stay strong. These whispers are just trying to break our spirit."

Zara nodded, determination evident in her eyes. "We won't let them. We have to save Alice."

As they drew closer to the lantern, a figure emerged from the shadows. It was a woman, her face obscured by a dark veil. In her hand, she held a chain, at the end of which was a cage. And within that cage, to the group's horror, was Alice.

Zara gasped, taking a step back. "Alice!"

The veiled woman chuckled, her voice cold and mocking. "Looking for someone?"

Kai took a defiant step forward. "Release her. Now."

The woman tilted her head, her unseen eyes studying the trio. "Why should I? She's mine now."

The Keeper, his voice calm but firm, replied, "She doesn't belong to you. We won't leave without her."

The veiled woman laughed, a sound that sent chills down their spines. "Very well. But if you want her, you'll have to play a little game."

Zara, her patience wearing thin, snapped, "Enough of these games! Just let her go!"

The woman sighed, a hint of amusement in her voice. "It's simple, really. Each of you will face a test. Pass, and Alice is yours. Fail, and she stays with me. Forever."

The Keeper frowned, considering the woman's words. "And what are these tests?"

The veiled woman smirked. "You'll see. Let's begin, shall we?"

Without warning, the world around them shifted. The desolate plain gave way to a bustling city street. Kai found himself standing alone, surrounded by a sea of unfamiliar faces. Panic welled up inside him, but he took a deep breath, reminding himself that this was just a test.

Suddenly, a voice echoed in his ears. *"Find the one who doesn't belong."*

Kai looked around, trying to spot anything out of place. And then he saw her. A young girl, no older than ten, sitting alone on a bench. Her clothes were tattered, and her eyes held a look of deep sadness.

Without hesitation, Kai approached the girl. "Are you okay?"

The girl looked up, her eyes filled with tears. "I'm lost. Can you help me?"

Kai nodded, taking the girl's hand. "Of course. Let's find your family."

As they walked hand in hand, the city street faded, replaced by the desolate plain. Kai found himself back with Zara, the Keeper, and the veiled woman.

The woman, her voice dripping with disdain, said, "Well done. But that was just the beginning."

Zara stepped forward, her gaze fixed on the veiled woman. "I'm ready. Give me my test."

The woman smirked. "As you wish."

And with that, the world shifted once more.

Chapter 10: A Glimpse of Truth

The world around Zara warped and twisted, leaving her in a quaint little town that seemed oddly familiar. The streets were lined with white-picketed houses, children laughed as they rode their bicycles, and the air smelled of fresh apple pie. It was a scene straight out of a nostalgic memory.

She glanced around, trying to grasp the meaning of this test. A soft voice behind her whispered, "Find what's hidden in plain sight."

Spinning around, Zara found herself face to face with a woman in her early thirties, holding a basket filled with freshly baked goods. "Oh, hello dear," the woman said, smiling warmly. "You seem new here. Looking for something?"

Zara hesitated, then replied, "I think so. But I'm not entirely sure what."

The woman chuckled softly. "Aren't we all? Well, feel free to look around. Maybe you'll find what you're seeking."

As Zara wandered the streets, she was greeted by friendly faces, each person more pleasant than the last. But she felt a nagging sensation that something was amiss. She paused in front of a local bookstore, its windows displaying an array of classic novels.

A young boy, no more than eight years old, sat on the steps, reading intently. Zara approached him, curious. "What are you reading?"

The boy looked up, his hazel eyes twinkling. "It's a story about adventures, mysteries, and hidden truths."

Zara, intrigued, sat down next to him. "Hidden truths? Like what?"

The boy hesitated, then leaned in, whispering, "Like the fact that not everything in this town is as it seems."

Before Zara could ask more, a horn honked loudly. The boy jumped up, waving. "That's my ride! Remember, look beyond the obvious!" He handed Zara the book and dashed off.

Opening the book, Zara found a note: "To see the hidden, reflect on the truth."

Confused, she glanced around, her eyes landing on a nearby pond. She approached it and gazed into its clear waters. Her reflection stared back, but behind her, the town's picture-perfect image started to waver and change. The white-picketed houses appeared run-down, the children's laughter sounded more like cries, and the pleasant townspeople now had sorrowful expressions.

Heart pounding, Zara turned to confront the reality. The woman with the basket of baked goods now looked weary and overburdened. "You see it now, don't you?" she asked, her voice filled with sadness.

Zara nodded, her voice soft. "Why didn't you tell me?"

The woman sighed, "Sometimes, it's easier to live in a lie than face the truth."

The scene around Zara started to dissolve, bringing her back to the desolate plain with the veiled woman. The Keeper was next.

His surroundings changed to a grand library, with towering shelves filled with countless books. A deep voice echoed, "Knowledge is power. Find the book that holds the key."

The Keeper, always valuing knowledge, began his search. Hours seemed to pass, with no sign of the elusive book. Frustration mounted until he overheard two scholars in whispered conversation.

"It's said that the most powerful book isn't found on any shelf but is carried within someone's heart."

The Keeper approached a librarian, an elderly man with spectacles. "Excuse me, sir, do you have a book not on these shelves but carried within the heart?"

The librarian smiled, tapping his chest. "Ah, you seek the Book of Memories. Close your eyes and remember your most cherished moment."

The Keeper did, and when he opened his eyes, a glowing book lay before him. Its pages contained not words, but emotions, memories, and love. Realizing the book symbolized the power of human connections, he thanked the librarian, returning to the veiled woman.

The trio had passed their tests, but the veiled woman's laugh shattered their relief. "Did you think it would be that easy? Now, for the final test."

Suddenly, Alice's cage started to rise, floating higher and higher. "If you truly want her back," the veiled woman sneered, "you'll have to reach her."

The ground below them started to crumble, leaving only narrow pillars leading towards Alice.

Kai shouted, "We'll do whatever it takes!"

But as they started their treacherous path, a blinding light enveloped them, leaving the reader in suspense.

Chapter 11: On Pillars of Hope and Despair

The dazzling white light was blinding, and for a moment, all that existed was the sensation of falling. And then, just as suddenly as it had appeared, the light faded, revealing a landscape transformed. The previously crumbling ground had given way to an expanse of narrow, uneven pillars, each jutting up from a seemingly infinite abyss below.

Zara, Kai, and The Keeper found themselves separated, each standing on individual pillars, with the cage containing Alice floating tantalizingly out of reach in the distance. The chilling laughter of the veiled woman echoed in the void around them.

"Think of this as a game," her voice resonated, dripping with malice. "Reach Alice, if you can. But one wrong step, one falter, and into the abyss you'll fall."

Zara felt a surge of anger. "You won't get away with this," she yelled into the void, her voice echoing back.

The veiled woman's laughter only grew louder. "Let's see if your confidence remains once the game truly begins."

Suddenly, the pillars began to shift, moving up and down, some tilting precariously. Zara could hear the distant shouts of Kai and The Keeper, but she couldn't see them; they were obscured by the maze of moving stone.

Taking a deep breath, she mustered her courage and made a leap to the next pillar. It wobbled under her weight, and for a heart-stopping second, she thought she would fall, but she managed to stabilize herself just in time.

As she progressed, jumping from pillar to pillar, she could hear Kai shouting words of encouragement. "You've got this, Zara! We're right behind you!"

Zara managed a smile, despite her fear. "Don't look down," she muttered to herself as she leaped again.

Meanwhile, The Keeper, relying on his wisdom and intuition, had started chanting incantations. With each word, a faint glow surrounded his feet, stabilizing the pillars as he moved. He was making steady progress.

Kai, with his innate agility, darted from one pillar to the next with relative ease. But he could see that further ahead, the pillars were even more unstable, some even crumbling as soon as they were touched.

He shouted a warning to the others, "Be careful! Some of these pillars are traps!"

Just as he finished his sentence, a pillar in front of Zara crumbled away, forcing her to leap backward to avoid plummeting into the abyss. She landed hard, scraping her hands, and for a moment, felt a pang of despair. But thinking of Alice, she picked herself up and continued forward, more cautiously this time.

The three of them communicated, shouting warnings and guiding each other. It was teamwork at its finest, each relying on the others' strengths.

After what felt like hours, they finally found themselves within arm's reach of Alice's cage. But as they prepared to free her, the voice of the veiled woman echoed once again.

"Congratulations on making it this far. But did you truly believe I'd make it so easy?"

Suddenly, the pillars beneath them began to shake violently. Zara grabbed onto the cage, desperately trying to maintain her balance. Kai and The Keeper tried to use their abilities to stabilize the ground, but it was no use.

As the world crumbled around them, a shadow emerged from the abyss, enveloping everything in its path. The veiled woman appeared, her form even more menacing.

"You have one choice," she hissed. "Give up now, or watch as I send your dear friend into the abyss."

The Keeper stepped forward, his voice firm. "Release her. This is between you and us. She has no part in this."

The veiled woman sneered. "Every story needs its sacrifices."

Zara, summoning strength she didn't know she had, shouted, "No! We won't let you!"

The atmosphere grew tense, the stakes higher than ever. And just when it seemed all hope was lost, a blinding light emerged from the cage, illuminating everything. As it faded, Alice stood outside the cage, her eyes glowing with an ethereal light.

"You underestimated the power of friendship and love," she whispered, her voice echoing with authority.

The veiled woman, taken aback, began to retreat. But before she could escape, Alice spoke a single word, causing chains of light to bind the villain.

However, the victory was short-lived as the ground began to rumble once again. The pillars, destabilized from the previous confrontations, started to collapse. The group, including a now-restrained veiled woman, found themselves plummeting into the abyss.

Zara's scream pierced the air as darkness enveloped them, leaving the fate of our heroes uncertain.

Chapter 12: Whispers in the Wind

The sensation of falling felt endless. Cold winds rushed past, and the only sound was the echo of their heartbeats. Suddenly, with a gentle lurch, they landed, not on hard ground, but on something soft and almost... feathery?

Zara blinked her eyes open. They were surrounded by a vast expanse of floating dandelions, their seeds drifting like a thick fog. They weren't in the abyss anymore. Instead, it seemed they had landed in some strange, ethereal meadow, suspended high above the world.

Alice, her ethereal glow now dimmed, was the first to speak. "Where are we?"

The Keeper, who seemed to be the least disoriented, replied, "It's the Meadow of Memories, a liminal space between worlds. But it shouldn't be accessible. Something is amiss."

Kai, brushing dandelion seeds off his clothes, squinted into the distance. "Do you see that? There's a figure standing over there."

The group turned to where Kai was pointing. In the midst of the dense dandelion fog, a silhouette stood. It was the veiled woman, but her demeanor was different—she looked lost and vulnerable without her menacing aura.

Zara took a cautious step forward. "Why did you bring us here?" she demanded.

The veiled woman looked up, her eyes vacant. "I... I didn't. This place... it's familiar, but I don't know why."

Alice, her voice gentle, approached the veiled woman. "You are trapped in your own memories. This place reflects that."

The veiled woman's eyes flickered with recognition. "I used to play here... as a child. Before everything changed." She seemed almost on the verge of tears.

Zara, seeing this vulnerability, felt her anger wane. "We need to get out of here. Can you help us?"

The veiled woman hesitated, then nodded. "There's a portal, but it's protected. We need to unlock it together."

Working in unison, they began searching for the portal. Along the way, memories flickered around them, almost like scenes from a movie. They witnessed the veiled woman's transformation—from a carefree child playing in the meadows to a bitter and vengeful sorceress.

"These memories... they're so sad," murmured Alice, tears in her eyes.

The veiled woman, watching her past play out, whispered, "I lost everything. My family, my home... I was consumed by anger and revenge."

Kai, usually so quick to judge, placed a comforting hand on her shoulder. "It's never too late to change."

They finally found the portal, a shimmering gateway surrounded by ancient runes. "Together," said The Keeper, and they all joined hands.

But as they approached, the portal repelled them, and an ominous voice boomed, "Only by confronting the past can one move forward."

Zara, taking a deep breath, said, "We need to face our memories, good and bad. Only then can we unlock the portal."

One by one, they stepped forward. Zara remembered her childhood, the love of her parents, and the pain of their loss. Kai remembered his struggles, his triumphs, and the lessons he had learned. The Keeper, ancient as he was, remembered countless moments, spanning centuries.

Finally, it was the veiled woman's turn. She hesitated, taking a shaky breath. "I don't know if I can."

Alice approached her, holding out her hand. "You don't have to do it alone."

With a nod, the veiled woman stepped forward. Her memories played out—love, loss, betrayal, and, ultimately, redemption.

As her memories faded, the portal glowed brighter, its barrier dissipating. Together, they stepped through, leaving the Meadow of Memories behind.

They found themselves back in their world, the sun shining brightly above. The veiled woman, her appearance transformed, looked around in wonder. "I... I remember now. My name is Lila."

Zara smiled. "Welcome back, Lila."

But their reunion was cut short as the ground trembled beneath them. A deep, echoing roar resonated, and from the horizon, a giant shadow approached, its eyes glowing red.

Lila's eyes widened in fear. "It's him. The one who started it all."

As the menacing figure drew closer, the world around them darkened, and the group braced themselves for the ultimate confrontation.

Chapter 13: Echoes of the Past

The sun had been radiant just moments before, but now, a shadow loomed, blanketing the landscape in an eerie half-light. The looming figure drew closer, its gargantuan silhouette stretching over the hills and valleys, swallowing everything in its path.

Lila, her newly remembered identity still fresh, whispered, "It's Malachi, the dark sorcerer. He was once my mentor."

Kai, squinting into the distance, said, "He seems... unnatural. Not just in size but in presence."

Zara, ever the protector, placed herself in front of the group. "How do we stop him?"

Lila closed her eyes briefly, trying to pull memories from the depths of her consciousness. "I don't know... but there is something... a relic that could counteract his power."

Alice, the ethereal guide who had been with them through thick and thin, murmured, "The Orb of Lumina. It's said to balance the darkest of magics."

Zara turned sharply, "Why didn't you mention this before?"

Alice looked apologetic. "I wasn't sure it was real. It's a legend, a story passed down through generations."

The Keeper, ancient eyes watchful, chimed in, "Legends often have a kernel of truth. We must find this Orb."

Lila hesitated before speaking, "I remember a clue from my training with Malachi. 'In the heart of the mountain, where shadows meet light, the Orb's power shines ever bright.'"

Kai clapped his hands together, "Well, that's helpful! A mountain. Because there are so few of those around."

Ignoring Kai's sarcasm, Zara thought aloud, "Shadows meet light... It could mean a cave or cavern within a mountain. A place where daylight seeps in."

The group set off, the shadow of Malachi always in the backdrop, his presence a constant reminder of the urgency of their quest. As they journeyed, the landscape shifted, from rolling hills to rocky terrain and finally to the foot of a majestic mountain range.

After hours of searching, they found a cavern entrance, with light filtering through cracks in the ceiling, creating a mesmerizing dance of shadows.

Lila hesitated at the entrance, her face pale. "This place... it's familiar. I trained here, long ago."

Alice gently squeezed Lila's hand. "It's okay. We're with you."

Venturing deeper into the cavern, they encountered challenges that tested their wit, strength, and teamwork. From riddles carved into ancient stone to traps designed to deter intruders, they relied on each other more than ever.

At the heart of the cavern, they found a chamber bathed in a soft, golden glow. In the center stood a pedestal, and atop it rested a radiant orb.

Lila approached it cautiously, "The Orb of Lumina."

Zara, looking around the chamber, said, "It seems too easy. No guards, no final test?"

Just as the words left her mouth, the ground shook, and a barrier formed around the Orb, trapping it within.

Kai groaned, "You had to jinx it, didn't you?"

From the shadows emerged a figure, a guardian of the Orb. It wasn't a creature of flesh and blood but a spectral entity, its form constantly shifting.

"You who seek the Orb," it intoned, "must prove your worth. Why do you desire its power?"

Lila stepped forward, "We seek to balance the darkness that threatens our world. To stop a power that was wrongly unleashed."

The guardian studied her, its form momentarily stabilizing into that of an elderly, wise-looking man. "And what of your intentions, Lila? Once a pupil of the very power you now oppose?"

Lila swallowed hard, "I was lost, but now I seek redemption. The Orb isn't for me, but for the world we wish to save."

The guardian turned its gaze to each member of the group, seemingly peering into their souls. After what felt like an eternity, the barrier around the Orb dissipated.

"Use it wisely," the guardian whispered before fading away.

With the Orb in their possession, the group hurried back to confront Malachi. As they emerged from the cavern, the dark sorcerer's presence was even more oppressive, his shadow nearly upon them.

Lila, holding the Orb, shouted, "Malachi, your reign of darkness ends now!"

The dark sorcerer laughed, a sound that sent shivers down their spines. "Do you really think that relic can stop me?"

The two forces collided, light against dark, in a spectacle of magic and power. The ground trembled, and the skies roared. Lila, channeling the Orb's power, became the beacon of hope, while the rest of the group provided support, battling Malachi's minions.

In the climax of their battle, just as victory seemed within reach, Malachi unleashed a spell that sent a blinding light towards Lila. But just before it could hit her, Alice, in a selfless act, jumped in front, absorbing the blast.

The aftermath was silent. Alice lay motionless on the ground, her ethereal glow dimmed. Lila, grief-stricken, unleashed a wave of power that finally overcame Malachi, banishing him and his shadow.

The group rushed to Alice's side, but she was fading fast. With a weak smile, she whispered, "It was always meant to be this way."

"No," Lila sobbed, "Not like this."

Alice's hand reached up to touch Lila's cheek. "Remember the balance. Light and dark. I'll always be with you."

And with that, Alice's form dissipated, leaving the group in stunned silence, the weight of their victory overshadowed by their loss.

Chapter 14: A Glimmer in the Gloom

The dust settled, a fine mist of sorrow settled on the group. The once formidable mountain range that echoed their adventures now stood as a silent testament to their grief. The sun was setting, casting a golden hue on everything, making the scene before them ironically beautiful. The juxtaposition of the warm light and their heavy hearts created a melancholic atmosphere.

Lila kneeled where Alice's ethereal form had disappeared, her hands touching the cold ground as if trying to feel the essence of their departed friend. Tears streamed down her face, their tracks visible on her dirt-streaked cheeks.

Kai, usually the voice of humor in the group, was uncharacteristically silent. He took off his hat, holding it to his chest, a gesture of respect for the departed.

Zara, her protective instinct kicking in, approached Lila and wrapped an arm around her. "It's okay to grieve," she whispered, her own voice thick with unshed tears.

Lila looked up, her blue eyes filled with pain. "I didn't... I couldn't save her."

The Keeper, who had seen countless lifetimes come and go, spoke with a gentle wisdom. "Life and death are two sides of the same coin, young one. Sometimes, despite our best efforts, we can't change fate."

Kai, clearing his throat, added, "Alice knew what she was doing. She saved us. She saved you, Lila."

Lila shook her head, "But at what cost?"

Before anyone could answer, a shimmering light caught their attention. From where Alice had vanished, a small crystalline pendant lay. It pulsed with a soft light, reminiscent of Alice's glow.

Zara picked it up, her fingers delicately cradling the pendant. "It's... It's Alice. Or at least, a part of her."

The Keeper leaned in, examining the pendant. "It's an echo. A fragment of her essence. It seems she left a piece of herself behind, for you."

Lila took the pendant, clutching it close to her heart. "Why would she do that?"

Kai offered, "Maybe as a way to remain with us? To guide us, like she always did."

As night enveloped them, the group set up camp, the warmth of the fire providing little comfort against their grief. They shared stories of Alice, each memory bringing both smiles and tears.

The Keeper recounted tales of the time Alice had guided a group of lost souls through the treacherous Forest of Whispers, while Kai fondly remembered the prank they played on a grumpy old troll, with Alice's ethereal glow turning the troll's hair pink.

The night deepened, and one by one, the group drifted off to sleep, the weight of the day's events taking its toll.

Lila, however, lay awake, the pendant's soft glow illuminating her face. Lost in thought, she didn't notice when it began to pulse brighter. A soft voice, eerily familiar, whispered in her ear, "Lila."

Startled, Lila sat up, looking around. "Alice? Is that you?"

The pendant floated up, the light shaping into a miniature form of Alice. "Yes, Lila. It's me."

Tears filled Lila's eyes. "I'm so sorry, Alice. I couldn't save you."

Alice's form smiled, "It was my choice, Lila. Don't blame yourself. I did what I had to do to protect all of you."

Lila whispered, "But why? Why did you have to leave us?"

Alice floated closer, her form touching Lila's cheek. "Sometimes, sacrifices are necessary for the greater good. Remember our purpose, Lila. You must continue the journey."

Lila nodded, "I will, Alice. For you."

Alice's form began to fade, "Remember, I'm always with you, in here," pointing towards Lila's heart.

As dawn approached, the group packed their belongings, ready to continue their quest. The weight of Alice's loss still heavy on their hearts, but with renewed determination.

As they journeyed, they came across a seemingly insurmountable obstacle, a chasm with no visible means of crossing. As they pondered their next move, a group of shadowy figures emerged from the other side, their intentions clearly hostile.

Zara stepped forward, weapons at the ready. "Looks like we have company."

Kai gulped, "And not the friendly kind."

Lila, clutching the pendant, whispered, "Alice, we need your guidance."

Suddenly, the pendant pulsed, and a bridge of light appeared, connecting the two sides of the chasm. The group hurried across, the shadowy figures hesitating at the unexpected turn of events.

Once they were safely on the other side, the bridge disappeared, leaving the figures stranded.

Kai let out a whoop, "Way to go, Alice!"

But their relief was short-lived. From the forest ahead, an even larger group of foes emerged, led by a figure that made Lila's blood run cold. It was Malachi, but different, more powerful.

He smirked, "Did you really think you could escape me, Lila? This ends now."

And with that, he unleashed a force that hurtled towards the group, the world fading to black.

Chapter 15: Fragments of the Past

Lila's head throbbed. The world around her was a swirl of muted colors and whispered voices. As her vision cleared, she found herself in a small, unfamiliar room with stone walls and minimal furnishing.

Kai was beside her, still unconscious, while Zara paced restlessly, glancing every so often out a small barred window. The Keeper sat cross-legged in a corner, deep in thought.

Lila tried to sit up but a wave of dizziness forced her back down. "Where are we?"

Zara rushed to her side, helping her sit up. "In Malachi's fortress. After his attack, we were captured."

Lila's heart raced. "Is everyone okay?"

Zara nodded, her expression grim. "We're all alive, for now. But there's no telling what Malachi has planned."

Lila clutched the pendant, feeling its familiar warmth. "We need to find a way out."

The Keeper, his voice resonating with wisdom, said, "Malachi's power has grown. The pendant alone may not be enough."

Lila's eyes glistened with determination. "We have each other. And Alice's essence. We won't give up."

Kai stirred, groaning. "Feels like I've been hit by a troll."

Zara smirked. "Close enough."

The atmosphere, though tense, was broken by a soft laughter. The camaraderie between them was palpable. But their moment of respite was short-lived.

The door swung open, revealing Malachi. His appearance was drastically changed - his eyes glowed an eerie blue, and dark veins streaked his face.

"Ah, awake at last," he sneered, his gaze fixed on Lila. "Did you really think you could defy me?"

Lila met his gaze defiantly. "As long as I breathe, I'll stand against you."

Malachi chuckled. "Brave words, but they won't save you."

Kai, ever the defiant one, quipped, "You might have the creepy fortress and the overdone villain look, but you're still the same old Malachi."

Malachi's face twisted in anger, but he restrained himself. "Enjoy your false bravado. It won't last long."

As he exited the room, the Keeper whispered, "He's drawing power from something. We need to find out what."

Zara nodded. "We need a plan. And fast."

Night fell, and with it came an eerie silence. The pendant glowed brighter, casting a soft illumination in the room.

Lila whispered, "Alice, if there's ever a time we need your guidance, it's now."

The pendant pulsed, and once again, Alice's form materialized. "Lila, you need to reach the heart of the fortress. Malachi has an artifact amplifying his power."

Lila's eyes widened. "An artifact? What is it?"

Alice replied, "A gemstone, forged in the heart of the ancient mountains. It taps into the ley lines of the world, channeling raw magic."

Kai, awed, said, "That sounds... powerful."

Alice nodded. "It is. But its power is unstable. You need to destroy it."

Zara interjected, "How? We're trapped here."

Alice smiled. "Remember our adventures? There's always a way."

With those words, the pendant dimmed, leaving the group in thoughtful silence.

Kai, breaking the tension, said, "Alright. Let's do what we do best - cause trouble."

Zara grinned. "I've been itching for some action."

The Keeper, deep in thought, said, "The artifact is bound to be heavily guarded. We'll need a diversion."

Lila, clutching the pendant, said, "Leave that to me."

The next hours were a blur of whispered plans and silent moves. Using a combination of stealth and cunning, they managed to navigate the labyrinthine corridors of the fortress.

As they neared the heart of the fortress, the energy in the air grew palpable. The artifact's power was evident.

Finally, they reached a grand chamber, in the center of which stood a pedestal, atop which rested the gemstone, pulsing with an inner light.

Kai whistled. "That's... shiny."

Lila approached it cautiously. "We need to destroy it."

The Keeper warned, "Be careful. Its power is immense."

Just as Lila was about to touch the gemstone, a voice echoed through the chamber, "Did you really think it would be that easy?"

Malachi appeared, his form even more formidable. The chamber was instantly filled with shadowy figures, ready for a fight.

Zara, weapons drawn, said, "Let's dance."

What followed was a fierce battle, a blend of magic and might. Every time one of the shadowy figures was defeated, another took its place.

Amidst the chaos, Lila made her way to the gemstone, the pendant glowing fiercely. As she touched the gemstone, a surge of energy coursed through her. The world around her blurred, and she found herself in a different place.

She was in a lush forest, the sounds of nature all around. But this tranquility was broken by a familiar voice, "Lila."

She turned to see a younger Malachi, his appearance normal, his eyes filled with sadness.

Lila, confused, asked, "Where am I? What is this?"

Malachi replied, "A fragment of the past. Before power corrupted me."

Lila took a step back. "Why show me this?"

Malachi, his voice filled with regret, said, "To show you that there's still a chance. A chance to save me."

Lila, tears in her eyes, whispered, "How?"

Malachi took a deep breath. "Destroy the gemstone. Free me from its grasp."

The world around Lila started to fade, the sounds of the battle growing louder. As she reappeared in the chamber, she knew what she had to do.

With newfound determination, she channeled all her energy, along with the pendant's power, into the gemstone. There was a blinding flash, and then silence.

The chamber was empty, save for the group, panting and exhausted. The gemstone lay shattered.

Kai, catching his breath, said, "That was... intense."

Zara nodded, "But we did it."

The Keeper, looking around, said, "The fortress is crumbling. We need to leave."

As they made their way out, Lila couldn't shake off the feeling that something was amiss. As they emerged into the daylight, a shadow loomed over them.

Malachi stood there, his appearance normal, but his eyes... They were empty, devoid of any emotion.

Lila approached him cautiously. "Malachi?"

He looked at her, his voice cold, "You may have destroyed the gemstone, but the power... it's still within me."

And with those chilling words, he vanished, leaving the group in stunned silence.

Kai, breaking the silence, said, "What just happened?"

Lila, her voice trembling, replied, "I think... I think we've just unleashed something even more dangerous."

Chapter 16: Unraveling Threads

The sun dipped behind the horizon, painting the sky in hues of purple and gold. But its beauty was lost on the group, each of them weighed down by the events of the day. The fortress, once an imposing structure, was now reduced to rubble, a testament to the power they had unleashed.

Lila sat on a fallen log, her thoughts a whirlwind. The pendant, which had always been a source of comfort, now felt heavy around her neck. "Did we do the right thing?" she murmured, mostly to herself.

Kai, ever the pillar of support, sat next to her. "Lila, we did what we had to. None of us could've predicted the outcome."

Zara, joining them, added, "Malachi's transformation... it's beyond anything we've faced before."

The Keeper, gazing at the remnants of the fortress, said, "This is merely a beginning. The power within Malachi, though dormant, has been awakened. And it seeks an outlet."

Lila looked up, her eyes filled with determination. "Then we find a way to stop it. Permanently."

Zara nodded. "But how? The gemstone was our only lead."

The Keeper, his voice contemplative, said, "There are ancient scrolls, hidden away in the Library of Eldoria. They might hold the key."

Kai raised an eyebrow. "Library of Eldoria? Sounds fancy."

The Keeper chuckled, "It is one of the oldest repositories of knowledge in our realm. But accessing it won't be easy."

Lila, curiosity piqued, asked, "Why?"

The Keeper replied, "The library is guarded by the Elders. They do not take kindly to outsiders."

Zara smirked, "Well, they haven't met us yet."

Kai, trying to lighten the mood, added, "Besides, how tough can a bunch of old librarians be?"

The Keeper, smiling, said, "You'd be surprised."

As night deepened, they set up camp, the fire's warmth a stark contrast to the chill in the air. Each of them lost in their thoughts, the weight of their mission pressing down on them.

The next morning, after a hearty breakfast, they set off towards Eldoria. The journey was long and arduous, taking them through dense forests and treacherous mountain paths. But their determination was unwavering.

One evening, as they sat around the campfire, Zara, her voice hesitant, said, "There's something I haven't told you all."

Lila, concerned, asked, "What is it?"

Zara took a deep breath. "My grandmother... she was an Elder."

The group exchanged surprised glances. Kai, trying to lighten the mood, said, "Well, that explains a lot."

Zara, smiling, replied, "Very funny. But it might give us an advantage."

The Keeper nodded. "Indeed. But we must tread carefully. The Elders are bound by traditions, and they do not take kindly to change."

As they neared Eldoria, the landscape changed. The dense forests gave way to rolling meadows, dotted with clusters of ancient trees. The air was filled with a sense of timelessness.

Finally, after what felt like an eternity, they reached the Library of Eldoria. It was a magnificent structure, its walls covered in intricate carvings, each telling a story from a bygone era.

They were met by a group of Elders, their appearance belying their age. Their leader, a tall, regal woman, stepped forward. "State your purpose."

Lila, taking a deep breath, said, "We seek knowledge. Knowledge to stop a power that threatens our very existence."

The leader, her gaze piercing, replied, "Many have come before you, seeking knowledge for personal gain. What makes you different?"

Zara, stepping forward, said, "Eldria, it's me. Zara."

Eldria, her expression softening, said, "Ah, my granddaughter. You've grown."

Zara, her voice choked with emotion, replied, "It's been too long."

Eldria nodded. "Indeed. But the past is in the past. What do you seek?"

Lila, her voice firm, said, "We need to access the ancient scrolls. Time is of the essence."

Eldria, after a moment's hesitation, said, "Very well. But be warned, the knowledge within can be a double-edged sword."

As they entered the library, Lila was awestruck. Shelves upon shelves of ancient scrolls and books stretched as far as the eye could see.

With Eldria leading the way, they made their way to a secluded section. She handed Lila a scroll, its parchment yellowed with age. "This might hold the answers you seek."

Lila, carefully unrolling the scroll, began to read. The words, though ancient, resonated with a sense of urgency. It spoke of a power, ancient and untamed, that could either be a boon or a curse. The key to controlling it lay in balancing the elements.

Kai, peering over her shoulder, said, "Elements? Like fire, water, air, and earth?"

Lila nodded. "Exactly. But there's more. The power can only be controlled by someone pure of heart."

The Keeper, his voice grave, said, "That is a tall order. Purity of heart is a rarity."

Lila, her determination unwavering, said, "Then we find that person. No matter what it takes."

As they prepared to leave, Eldria approached Zara. "Promise me you'll be careful."

Zara, hugging her grandmother, replied, "I promise."

As they stepped out of the library, the sun setting in the distance, they were met by an unexpected sight. Malachi stood there, his aura pulsating with power.

Lila, her voice firm, said, "Malachi, we don't want to hurt you."

Malachi, his voice cold, replied, "The feeling isn't mutual."

And with those chilling words, he unleashed a burst of energy, sending the group flying.

As they struggled to their feet, Malachi, his voice dripping with malice, said, "You may have the knowledge, but I have the power."

And just as he was about to strike, a mysterious figure stepped in, blocking his path. The figure, hooded and cloaked, said, "Enough."

Malachi, taken aback, said, "Who are you?"

The figure, slowly lowering the hood, revealed a face that was all too familiar. It was Elara, Lila's mother, believed to have been lost years ago.

The group, in shock, could only stare as Elara, her voice filled with authority, said, "Malachi, stand down."

Malachi, his expression one of disbelief, said, "Elara? But you... you were supposed to be dead."

Elara, her gaze unwavering, replied, "Things aren't always as they seem."

Chapter 17: Echoes of the Past

The wind rustled gently, bringing with it the faint scent of roses. Eldoria's vast meadow, bathed in the soft glow of twilight, seemed like a painting. But the serene atmosphere was shattered by the standoff.

Elara, with an air of authority, confronted Malachi. "It's time to stop this madness," she said, her voice laced with a strength Lila had never heard before.

Malachi laughed bitterly. "Oh, Elara. The years haven't dulled your arrogance. But you're mistaken if you think you can stop me."

Zara, ever protective of her friends, stepped forward, "We won't let you harm anyone else."

Malachi glanced at her dismissively. "You? Protect? Don't make me laugh."

Kai, with a determined look, added, "You might have power, but we have something you'll never understand: unity and the will to protect."

The tension was palpable. The Keeper, always the voice of reason, said, "This isn't the way. Malachi, let's find another solution."

Malachi smirked. "I am the solution."

As Lila watched the exchange, she felt a mix of emotions. Fear, certainly, but also an overwhelming urge to protect her mother, to make up for the lost years. "Mom," she whispered, "how is this possible?"

Elara turned to face her daughter, her eyes glistening with tears. "Lila, there's so much I need to tell you."

Without warning, Malachi launched a powerful spell, targeting Elara. In an act of pure maternal instinct, she shielded Lila, absorbing the brunt of the attack. The force threw her several feet back, and she landed with a sickening thud.

"NO!" Lila screamed, rushing to her mother's side.

The group quickly formed a protective circle around Elara and Lila, ready to fend off any further attacks. But Malachi, for reasons unknown, simply watched, a strange, almost regretful look on his face.

Kai, Zara, and The Keeper focused their energy to create a barrier, ensuring Malachi couldn't get any closer.

Lila, tears streaming down her face, cradled her mother. "Please, Mom, you have to be okay."

Elara, weakly smiling, whispered, "I've missed you, my brave girl."

Zara, glancing anxiously at Malachi, said, "We need to get her to safety."

The Keeper nodded. "I know a place."

With Kai and Zara supporting Elara, the group quickly retreated, leaving behind a contemplative Malachi.

They reached a secluded glen, its tranquility a stark contrast to the earlier chaos. A crystal-clear stream flowed nearby, its gentle gurgle soothing.

Laying Elara on a soft patch of grass, Lila asked, "Keeper, can you help her?"

The Keeper, deeply concentrating, replied, "I'll try." He began chanting an ancient spell, his hands glowing with a soft light as he placed them over Elara.

Minutes felt like hours. Finally, The Keeper, exhaustion evident, said, "It's done. She'll recover, but it'll take time."

Lila, relief washing over her, said, "Thank you."

Kai, rubbing his temples, said, "That was too close. Malachi's power has grown."

Zara, her eyes focused on the horizon, replied, "And it's only going to get worse."

The Keeper, deep in thought, added, "There's more to Malachi than meets the eye. His connection to Elara, it's personal."

Lila, curiosity piqued, asked, "What do you mean?"

Elara, her voice weak but steady, replied, "Malachi and I... we have a history."

The group exchanged glances. Lila, her voice barely above a whisper, said, "Tell us."

Elara took a deep breath. "Years ago, Malachi and I trained together, under the tutelage of the great sorcerer, Eldran. We were close, perhaps too close."

Zara, realization dawning, said, "You loved him."

Elara nodded. "Yes, but it was a complicated love. Power, ambition, it changed him. And when I chose a different path, a family, he couldn't accept it."

Lila, tears in her eyes, said, "He hurt you because of me?"

Elara, cupping her daughter's face, replied, "No, my love. It was never about you. It was about choices and the paths we choose."

The night deepened, the sky a tapestry of stars. They sat in silence, each lost in their thoughts.

Kai, breaking the silence, said, "We need a plan."

The Keeper, nodding in agreement, replied, "Yes, but first, we need information. We need to understand the extent of Malachi's power and his intentions."

Zara, determination in her voice, said, "Then let's get started."

Days turned into weeks. They researched, trained, and prepared. But as they delved deeper, they realized the magnitude of the challenge ahead.

One evening, as Lila was poring over an ancient text, she

stumbled upon a prophecy. "When darkness rises, and hope seems lost, a bond once broken will be the cost. But from the ashes, love will rise, uniting foes and severing ties."

Zara, intrigued, asked, "What does it mean?"

Lila, deep in thought, replied, "I'm not sure, but I have a feeling it's connected to my mom and Malachi."

The Keeper, contemplatively, said, "Prophecies are tricky. They're never straightforward."

Kai, a hint of frustration in his voice, said, "Then we need to decode it, and fast."

The next day, as they were training, they were interrupted by an unexpected visitor. A raven, black as night, landed gracefully, a note tied to its leg.

Lila cautiously approached, retrieving the note. Unfolding it, she read aloud, "Meet me at Eldoria's peak, at midnight."

The note was unsigned, but they all knew who it was from: Malachi.

The group exchanged worried glances. Lila, determination evident, said, "I'm going."

Kai, concern in his voice, replied, "It could be a trap."

Lila, resolutely, said, "I know. But it's a risk I'm willing to take."

The Keeper, gravely, added, "Be prepared for anything."

Night fell, and Lila, accompanied by Zara and Kai, made her way to Eldoria's peak. The moon, full and bright, illuminated their path.

As they reached the summit, they were met by Malachi, his silhouette menacing against the moonlit sky.

Lila, her voice firm, said, "I'm here. Now what?"

Malachi, his voice dripping with malice, replied, "It's time to finish what we started."

And just as he was about to strike, a powerful force intervened, separating the two.

The group, in shock, turned to see the source: Elara, her power fully awakened, ready to confront her past and protect her future.

Chapter 18: Unveiled Truths

Eldoria's peak stood majestic under the shimmering moonlight. Elara, with a newfound strength emanating from her, faced Malachi, her eyes glowing fiercely.

"You've become strong," Malachi remarked, not in mockery, but in what seemed like genuine surprise.

Elara responded, her voice carrying an edge, "It's not strength, Malachi. It's the power of love, of protection. Something you seem to have forgotten."

Malachi's expression shifted to one of sadness. "Elara, you know this isn't personal. This was never about you and me. It's about a world that needs to be reshaped."

Lila watched intently, trying to grasp the dynamics of their relationship. The air was thick with tension, emotions swirling like a storm.

Kai, sensing an impending confrontation, whispered to Zara, "We should be ready."

She nodded, her hand discreetly moving to her pocket where she had kept a vial of protective potion.

Lila, feeling a tug on her sleeve, turned to find The Keeper. "Lila," he whispered, "No matter what happens, remember the prophecy."

"I don't even fully understand it," Lila admitted, feeling overwhelmed.

"It will become clear in time. Just trust in your instincts."

As the two former lovers continued their exchange, their past unraveled.

Elara's voice softened. "Malachi, we trained together, dreamt together. We wanted to make the world better, together. But your idea of 'better' became twisted."

"I've seen the world, Elara," Malachi countered, "The chaos, the suffering. It needs order, and I can provide that."

"By subjugating everyone? By robbing them of their free will?"

Malachi's eyes darkened. "If that's what it takes."

Lila couldn't take it any longer. "Why did you hurt my mother? Why are you doing all this?"

Malachi's gaze shifted to Lila. "You're just like her. So full of fire." He sighed. "I didn't want to hurt Elara. But she chose a different path. One that took her away from me."

Elara interjected, "Life is about choices, Malachi. I chose love, family. And I don't regret it."

Malachi looked away, the weight of their history pressing down on him. "I loved you, Elara. And in my own twisted way, I still do. But I can't let that stop me."

The atmosphere was electric. It was evident that the next few moments would shape the fate of Eldoria.

Suddenly, the peak trembled, a forceful vibration that seemed to come from deep within. From the center of the summit, a fissure appeared, emitting a radiant blue glow.

Zara, her voice shaky, said, "That's... that's not natural."

The Keeper, with a sense of urgency, said, "The heart of Eldoria. It's awakening!"

Lila, confused, asked, "The what?"

Elara explained, "Eldoria's heart is a powerful crystal, hidden deep within this peak. Legend says it holds immense power."

Malachi's eyes gleamed. "The final piece," he whispered, almost to himself.

Kai, realizing Malachi's intent, exclaimed, "We can't let him get to it!"

The ground continued to rumble, the fissure widening, revealing the heart – a massive, pulsating crystal.

Malachi, with newfound determination, began chanting a spell, his hands weaving intricate patterns in the air.

Elara, recognizing the chant, cried out, "No! That's a binding spell!"

The Keeper, horror evident on his face, added, "He intends to bind himself to the heart, to harness its power!"

Lila, fear gripping her, said, "We have to stop him!"

Zara, quickly formulating a plan, said, "Kai, Lila, distract him. Keeper and I will work on a counter-spell."

As Kai and Lila engaged Malachi, Zara and The Keeper began their incantation. Their voices harmonized, producing a haunting melody that seemed to resonate with the very soul of Eldoria.

Malachi, feeling the pushback, roared in frustration. "You cannot stop me!"

Lila, summoning all her courage, shouted, "Watch us!"

The air crackled with magic. Spells clashed, creating brilliant displays of light and shadow. The fate of Eldoria hung in the balance.

Then, in a heart-stopping moment, Elara stepped in between Malachi and the heart, her arms spread out in a protective stance.

"Malachi," she cried, her voice filled with desperation and love, "Stop this! Remember us. Remember who you were."

Malachi, momentarily distracted, locked eyes with Elara. Memories flashed – of laughter, of love, of dreams shared. Tears formed, rolling down his cheeks.

But it was momentary. With a heart-wrenching scream, Malachi unleashed a surge of magic, targeting Elara. But just as it was about to hit her, Lila, driven by love and desperation, jumped in its path.

A blinding light engulfed the peak. And when it subsided, Lila lay on the ground, unconscious, with Elara cradling her, tears streaming.

The heart of Eldoria dimmed, its glow fading. Malachi, looking at what he'd done, screamed, a sound filled with pain and regret. And with a final burst of magic, he disappeared.

The night, which had witnessed so much, was now silent. The fate of Lila, the next Guardian of Eldoria, was uncertain, leaving everyone with a looming question - would she ever wake up?

Chapter 19: Echoes of Time

The gentle rays of dawn began to paint Eldoria's peak in hues of gold and pink, but the serene beauty was lost on the group. The silence that had settled was thick with shock, grief, and the aftermath of the magical duel that had just transpired.

Elara, still holding her daughter close, whispered words of comfort, her tears wetting Lila's face. "Come back to me," she murmured, her voice broken with emotion.

Zara and Kai stood a little distance away, lost in their own thoughts. The former's eyes were focused on the now dimmed heart of Eldoria, while Kai's gaze was on the horizon, as if expecting Malachi to return.

The Keeper, ever the calm presence, approached Elara. "We need to get her to the Sanctuary," he said softly, "Its waters might hold the power to heal her."

Elara nodded weakly, gently lifting Lila into her arms.

As they began their descent, Kai, trying to understand the events that had unfolded, voiced his confusion. "Why did Malachi leave? He was so close to getting what he wanted."

Zara, her mind racing with a million thoughts, replied, "Regret, perhaps? Seeing Lila's sacrifice might have triggered something inside him."

The Keeper, ever the source of wisdom, interjected, "The heart of Eldoria reflects the soul. Its fading light could be indicative of the turmoil inside Malachi."

Their journey to the Sanctuary was filled with quiet contemplation, each lost in their thoughts, pondering the weight of the choices they'd made and the consequences that lay ahead.

As they approached the Sanctuary, the still waters shimmered invitingly. Elara, with utmost care, placed Lila near the water's edge.

The Keeper began an ancient chant, his voice echoing through the serene surroundings. Slowly, Lila began to levitate, surrounded by a soft blue glow. The waters of the Sanctuary started to ripple, responding to The Keeper's call.

Elara watched, hope and fear warring in her eyes. "Please," she whispered, "Bring her back to me."

Time seemed to stretch endlessly, the silence broken only by The Keeper's melodic chant and the gentle lapping of the waters. Then, without warning, Lila's body was submerged.

Zara, ever the protective friend, reached out, but Kai held her back. "Trust the process," he murmured.

Minutes felt like hours. And just as despair was about to take hold, the waters calmed, and Lila floated back up, looking serene, as if asleep.

But her eyes remained closed.

Elara, her heart heavy, cradled Lila once again. "Why isn't she waking up?" Her voice, filled with anguish, echoed in the stillness.

The Keeper, looking grave, said, "The physical injuries have healed. But her spirit, it seems, is lost somewhere."

Kai, trying to grasp the gravity of the situation, questioned, "You mean, she's in some sort of limbo?"

Zara, tears forming, added, "Can we bring her back?"

The Keeper looked thoughtful. "There might be a way. But it's risky."

Elara, her voice firm, said, "Tell me. I'll do anything."

"The Astral Plains," began The Keeper, "is a realm where spirits wander. It's possible Lila's spirit is trapped there."

Zara, always curious, inquired, "How do we reach this place?"

"We don't," said The Keeper, "But Elara can. With the right guidance and incantation, she can project herself into the Astral Plains and find Lila."

Elara, without hesitation, responded, "Then let's begin."

As The Keeper prepared the ritual, Kai took Elara aside. "Are you sure about this? It's dangerous."

Elara, determination evident in her eyes, replied, "Lila sacrificed herself for me. I won't let her be lost."

The ritual was intricate. The Keeper chanted, using rare herbs to create a circle around Elara. The air grew thick with magic.

"Remember," warned The Keeper, "Time behaves differently in the Astral Plains. What feels like minutes could be hours or days here. Find Lila and bring her back quickly."

Elara nodded, taking a deep breath.

As the incantation reached its peak, Elara felt herself being pulled, her vision blurring. And then, she found herself in a vast, shimmering expanse. Ethereal figures floated around, their forms constantly shifting.

Elara began her search, calling out to Lila, her voice echoing. She encountered lost souls, each with their tales of love, loss, and regret.

Hours seemed to pass, but Lila was nowhere in sight. Doubt began to creep in. But just as despair threatened to take hold, a familiar voice whispered, "Mom?"

Turning around, Elara saw Lila, looking lost and confused. Their reunion was heartfelt, tears and smiles mingling.

"We need to leave," Elara said, her voice urgent.

Lila, looking around, replied, "I don't know the way back."

Taking her hand, Elara whispered words of an incantation The Keeper had taught her. Slowly, the ethereal world around them began to fade.

Chapter 20: The Heart's Veil

Eldoria's heart pulsed like an angry storm, its power casting eerie, dancing shadows that seemed to engulf the land in its dark embrace. The once tranquil Sanctuary now seemed a battlefield, charged with a palpable tension.

The group stood united, their faces a mix of determination and fear. Elara, with Lila by her side, seemed to gather strength from her daughter's presence. Zara and Kai stood slightly ahead, ready to defend against any immediate threat. And The Keeper, the wise sage, looked the most troubled of all.

"We were too late," murmured Zara, her grip on her staff tightening.

Kai, ever the optimist, replied, "We've faced bigger threats before."

But The Keeper's somber expression indicated otherwise. "The heart of Eldoria," he began, "was not just a source of magic, but it also kept a balance. With Malachi tapping into its core, that balance is threatened."

Elara, holding Lila close, spoke up, "So, what's our plan?"

Before anyone could answer, a chilling laughter echoed across the land. From the shadows emerged Malachi, his aura more menacing than ever.

"Did you truly think," he began, his voice dripping with condescension, "that you could stop me?"

Zara, her temper flaring, shot back, "We did once. We'll do it again."

Malachi's eyes glinted. "That was before I harnessed the true power of Eldoria. Now, it's a different game."

The tension was palpable, each side sizing up the other, waiting for the right moment to strike.

Suddenly, Malachi raised his hand, and dark tendrils of energy lashed out, targeting Lila.

Elara, her protective instincts kicking in, formed a protective shield around her daughter. "Stay away from her!"

But the onslaught continued, the dark energy threatening to shatter Elara's defenses.

Kai, sensing an opportunity, lunged at Malachi, his sword ablaze. A fierce duel ensued, with both opponents evenly matched. Every strike, every parry was charged with intensity.

Zara, using her magic, tried to divert some of Malachi's attention, casting spells that produced blinding flashes of light.

Amidst the chaos, The Keeper, using his deep knowledge of Eldoria's lore, began a counter incantation. His voice, though soft, carried a power that seemed to reverberate across the land.

Elara, though struggling, noticed The Keeper's efforts. "We need to buy him time," she whispered to Lila.

Lila, nodding, began to channel her own magic, amplifying her mother's shield.

The battle raged on. Zara and Kai, though valiant in their efforts, were slowly being overpowered. Malachi, with the heart of Eldoria fueling him, seemed unstoppable.

It was then that Lila, drawing upon a deep reservoir of untapped power, released a pulse of energy so powerful that it momentarily stunned Malachi.

Seizing the opportunity, Elara channeled her magic into a single, focused beam, targeting the heart of Eldoria.

There was a blinding flash of light, and when it cleared, the group found themselves in a different landscape. The heart of Eldoria stood untouched, but its surroundings had transformed. Lush meadows had replaced the rocky terrain, and a tranquil river flowed nearby.

Confused, Elara looked around. "Where are we?"

The Keeper, looking equally puzzled, replied, "It seems we've been transported to a different plane of Eldoria."

"But how?" inquired Zara.

Before they could ponder further, a gentle voice called out, "Welcome, brave ones."

Turning around, they saw a spectral figure, radiating a soft, ethereal glow. "I am Elda, the spirit of Eldoria," she said.

Elara, stepping forward, asked, "Why have you brought us here?"

Elda, her expression kind, replied, "To protect you. The heart sensed the danger and brought you to this safe haven."

The Keeper, always inquisitive, inquired, "But for how long? We can't stay here forever."

Elda nodded. "True. But while you're here, I can offer you knowledge. Knowledge that might help you counter Malachi's power."

The group listened intently as Elda recounted tales of ancient spells and artifacts that could potentially rival the heart's power.

As the conversation drew to a close, Kai, ever the practical one, voiced the question on everyone's mind, "How do we get back?"

Elda, with a sad smile, replied, "That is a journey you must undertake on your own. But remember the lessons learned here, and you might find a way."

With those parting words, she faded away, leaving the group with more questions than answers.

As they explored their new surroundings, trying to find a way back, they encountered various challenges. From solving intricate puzzles to battling shadowy creatures, their journey was fraught with danger.

But with each challenge, they grew stronger, their bonds deepening. And as days turned into weeks, they slowly began to uncover clues that hinted at a way back.

It was during one such exploration that Zara stumbled upon an ancient stone tablet. The inscriptions, though worn out, spoke of a portal that connected the different planes of Eldoria.

With renewed hope, they followed the clues,

which led them to a secluded cave. Inside, they found the portal, its surface shimmering with an otherworldly glow.

Elara, taking a deep breath, stepped forward. "It's time to face Malachi. Together."

As they stepped through the portal, they found themselves back in the heart of Eldoria. But things had changed. The land was desolate, and the once vibrant heart now pulsed with a sickly hue.

And waiting for them was Malachi, a triumphant smile on his face. "Welcome back," he sneered. "I've been expecting you."

The group braced themselves for the impending battle. But as they prepared, they noticed something. Malachi, though powerful, seemed different. The constant tapping into the heart's power had taken a toll on him.

Seizing the opportunity, they attacked, their combined strength overwhelming Malachi. But just as victory seemed imminent, Malachi, in a desperate move, unleashed the heart's full power.

The resulting explosion engulfed everything in its path. And when the dust settled, the group found themselves separated, each trapped in a different part of Eldoria.

Elara, dazed and confused, looked around. The heart, once a symbol of hope, now lay shattered. And with it, any hope of reuniting with her friends.

Just then, a familiar voice echoed, "Remember the lessons learned."

Turning around, she saw Elda's spectral figure. "Your journey has just begun," she said, her voice fading.

And as Elara looked around, trying to find a way out, she realized that the true battle for Eldoria had only just begun.

Chapter 21: Fractured Realms and Unseen Hands

As the dust settled around the destroyed heart of Eldoria, Elara's world seemed to spin. The verdant meadows that once flourished were now barren landscapes, and the harmonious tunes of nature were replaced by an eerie silence. Each member of the group, separated by an unfathomable force, found themselves in isolated pockets of Eldoria, worlds within a world.

Elara found herself amidst an overgrown forest, the trees reaching so high they seemed to touch the heavens. Beneath the trees, an underbrush full of thorns blocked her path. The place felt familiar, a distorted echo of the Eldoria she once knew.

"Lila?" she called out, her voice barely a whisper amidst the dense trees. But the forest only responded with its stillness. The haunting memory of Malachi's triumphant smirk sent shivers down her spine. Gathering herself, she trudged forward, cutting a path through the thorns.

A mile or so in, she encountered a stream with water so clear it mirrored the skies. As she bent down to drink, her reflection wavered, and another face appeared alongside hers - a younger, more innocent Elara, a memory from a time long past.

Tears welled up in her eyes. "Why am I seeing this now?" she murmured.

The reflection replied, "Because within you lies the strength you seek."

Elara jerked back, her heart racing. "Who are you?"

The reflection, with a mischievous smile reminiscent of Lila, replied, "A fragment of your past, and perhaps, a guide for your future."

Zara found herself in what looked like an endless maze of mirrors, each one reflecting a different version of herself. Some showed her as a powerful sorceress, others as a vulnerable child. But one mirror, in particular, stood out. It showed a version of Zara standing alongside Malachi, their hands entwined.

Staring at this image, she muttered, "That never happened."

A voice echoed from the mirrors, "But it could have. Each mirror shows a possibility, a path once considered."

Zara, her resolve firm, said, "I chose my path long ago. And it doesn't involve him."

The voice replied, "To find your way out, you must confront your deepest fears and embrace your true self."

Kai, on the other hand, was on a desolate battlefield. Ghostly apparitions of warriors past floated around, re-enacting battles from eons ago. Among them, he saw figures he recognized – old friends and mentors who had fallen.

"Is this the afterlife?" he wondered aloud.

One of the spirits, a former comrade, responded, "Not quite, young warrior. This is a realm where past battles continue to rage. A place of unresolved conflicts."

Kai, gripping his sword, said, "Then I will fight alongside my brothers once more and find my way back."

The Keeper, being the most attuned to the subtleties of Eldoria, found himself in a vast library, its shelves lined with ancient tomes and scrolls. A figure, hooded and draped in robes, approached him.

"You seek knowledge," it said.

The Keeper, always wary, replied, "I seek a way out."

The figure responded, "The two are not mutually exclusive."

Back in the forest, Elara's reflection provided her with clues. "To reunite with your friends, you must find the four elemental crystals scattered across this realm. Only when combined can they mend the heart of Eldoria."

As Elara continued her journey, she encountered various challenges – from deciphering riddles to battling forest creatures. But with each challenge, memories of her past adventures with her friends gave her strength.

In the mirror maze, Zara confronted her fears, shattering the mirrors that bound her to her doubts. With each shattered reflection, a path cleared, leading her closer to an exit.

On the battlefield, Kai fought valiantly, laying the restless spirits to rest. With each victory, a piece of the battlefield transformed, revealing patches of the Eldoria he remembered.

In the library, The Keeper delved deep into the lore of Eldoria, uncovering ancient rituals and spells. The hooded figure, watching from afar, whispered, "He is the key."

As the days turned into weeks, each member drew closer to their individual goals. Elara, with three crystals in her possession, stood at the edge of a cliff, the final crystal just out of reach on a distant peak.

As she pondered her next move, the ground shook, and the peak started to crumble. Desperate, Elara reached out, her magic intertwining with the crystal's energy. There was a blinding flash of light, and she found herself falling.

Meanwhile, as Zara neared the exit of the maze, the mirrors began to warp, their reflections turning grotesque. One, in particular, showed Malachi with a triumphant grin, Lila by his side. Zara, her heart heavy, ran towards the exit, but it seemed to move further away.

Kai, having transformed a majority of the battlefield, faced his final challenge. An apparition of himself, corrupted by darkness. The two clashed, their swords ringing out in the silent realm.

The Keeper, having gathered enough knowledge, began a ritual to reconnect the realms. But as he chanted, the hooded figure approached, its intentions unclear.

As Elara fell, she caught a glimpse

of Zara trapped in the mirrors and Kai battling his doppelganger. With newfound determination, she channeled her magic, creating a portal that linked their realms.

Suddenly, they all found themselves back in the heart of Eldoria, but not as they remembered it. The heart, though shattered, pulsed weakly, its light dim.

The hooded figure, now revealed to be an ancient guardian of Eldoria, approached. "You've done well," it said. "But the true test lies ahead."

Before they could react, the heart pulsed once more, its energy enveloping them. When the light faded, they found themselves in an alternate Eldoria, a world where Malachi ruled supreme.

And in the distance, Lila, now a powerful sorceress under Malachi's influence, awaited them.

Chapter 22: A Dance with Shadows

Eldoria's alternate landscape was as foreign as it was haunting. The once vibrant hues of the realm were now replaced with an almost monochrome palette. The air was thick, not with the fragrance of blooming flowers, but a smoky heaviness. Elara, Zara, Kai, and the Keeper gazed at the chilling sight of this new world, a twisted reflection of their home.

Kai, his warrior spirit ever-present, gripped his sword. "We need a plan. Malachi's influence is evident, and Lila..." His voice trailed off, thinking of their once cherished friend, now an adversary.

Zara, with a determined glint in her eyes, said, "We need to reach Lila. She's key to understanding this place. And perhaps, deep down, there's still a part of her that remembers us."

Elara nodded, "Agreed. But we need to be cautious. This Eldoria is unfamiliar, and we don't know what other changes Malachi has wrought."

As they strategized, they failed to notice the shadows gathering around them. Suddenly, one lunged at Elara, but Kai, always alert, swung his blade, dispersing it.

"These aren't ordinary shadows," the Keeper observed. "They're manifestations of Malachi's power. We must stay vigilant."

Navigating this gloomy terrain, the group encountered inhabitants who were mere shadows of their former selves, their spirits broken by Malachi's tyranny. It was a grim reminder of the stakes at hand.

After hours of careful journeying, they reached what appeared to be the central square. To their shock, they saw statues of themselves, commemorating their 'defeat' at Malachi's hands. The statues, eerily lifelike, bore expressions of despair.

Zara, her voice shaky, whispered, "This... this is a message. Malachi wants us to see this."

Before they could further process the unsettling sight, a familiar voice echoed through the square, "Impressive, isn't it?"

They turned to see Lila, but not the Lila they remembered. Her eyes, once full of mischief and warmth, now glowed with a cold fire. Dressed in dark robes, she looked every bit the powerful sorceress she had become.

Elara took a hesitant step forward, "Lila, it's us. Please, remember."

Lila chuckled, a sound devoid of its usual warmth. "Oh, I remember alright. And I've been waiting for this moment."

A tense silence enveloped the square. Zara finally spoke, "Why, Lila? Why side with Malachi?"

Lila smirked, "Power, dear Zara. The kind you couldn't even fathom."

Kai, his anger evident, growled, "You betray your friends for power?"

Lila's eyes flitted to Kai, her voice dripping with sarcasm, "Oh, Kai, always the noble warrior. Tell me, how does it feel to see your world, your friends, in ruins?"

The Keeper, ever the diplomat, interjected, "Lila, we're not here to fight. We want to understand, to help. Eldoria's heart can still be mended."

Lila tilted her head, considering his words. "Perhaps. But at what cost?" With a swift motion, she summoned a vortex, trapping the group.

Inside the vortex, time and reality were warped. Elara found herself back in the forest, but this time, she was alone, and the weight of her solitude was crushing. Zara was back in the mirror maze, the reflections now mocking her every move. Kai was once again on the battlefield, but instead of spectral adversaries, he faced the very real threat of his darkest fears. And the Keeper, trapped in the library, saw the tomes and scrolls turn to ash, symbolizing lost knowledge.

As despair threatened to consume them, a shared memory surfaced — of their first adventure together, a simpler time filled with laughter, camaraderie, and the promise of many journeys ahead. Drawing strength from this memory, each began to fight back against Lila's illusion.

Elara, summoning her innate magic, began to reconnect with the forest, making it an ally rather than an adversary. Zara, confronting each reflection, found the exit once more. Kai, realizing the battlefield was a construct of his mind, willed it to transform into the Eldoria he loved. The Keeper, using his vast knowledge, began rewriting the lost texts, restoring the library.

United in spirit, they managed to shatter Lila's vortex. Emerging back into the square, they faced Lila, who looked momentarily disoriented by their resilience.

Elara, her voice firm, declared, "Lila, this isn't you. You're stronger than Malachi's influence."

Lila hesitated, a flicker of doubt crossing her features. But before she could reply, a dark mist enveloped the square. From its depths, Malachi emerged.

"Well done, Lila," he sneered. "You've brought them right to me."

The group readied themselves for the battle ahead. But as they did, the ground beneath them began to tremble. From the shadows, monstrous creatures, amalgamations of Eldoria's worst nightmares, began to emerge, circling them.

The odds seemed insurmountable. Just as hope seemed lost, a soft glow emanated from Elara's amulet. It began to hum a familiar tune, one from their childhood.

Lila's eyes widened in recognition. Memories of their shared past began flooding back. The cold fire in her eyes was replaced by tears.

But would it be enough to turn the tide? As the monstrous horde closed in, the group, now potentially reunited with Lila, braced for the battle of their lives.

Chapter 23: Reunion and Revelations

The monstrous horde, a sight that would've struck terror in the bravest of hearts, descended upon our protagonists, their menacing forms contorting in the dim, smoky light. But this time, the team had an advantage they hadn't anticipated – Lila, their friend, potentially on their side once again.

As the monsters charged, the soft glow from Elara's amulet intensified, pushing back some of the encroaching darkness. It was as though the heart of Eldoria, that ancient magic, recognized one of its own and sought to protect.

Zara, her swift reflexes in play, danced between the creatures, her blade leaving a trail of light. Kai, ever the warrior, stood firm, his sword deflecting one attack after another.

Yet it was the transformation in Lila that was most profound. The memories triggered by the amulet's song had momentarily weakened Malachi's grip on her. She seemed torn, the internal battle evident in her eyes. The young sorceress, once brimming with ambition, now stood at a crossroads.

Elara approached her, dodging an oncoming creature. "Lila," she panted, "you have to fight it. Remember who you are, remember us."

Lila's eyes met Elara's, a myriad of emotions swirling within. "I...I remember," she whispered, tears streaming down her face. With newfound resolve, she raised her hands, casting a spell that held the monsters at bay.

Malachi, witnessing this rebellion, roared in fury. "You dare defy me, Lila?"

Lila, her voice steady, replied, "I'm not your puppet, Malachi. I remember everything."

But the evil sorcerer wasn't going to let her go easily. With a flick of his wrist, he summoned a cage of dark energy, trapping Lila within. "If you won't serve me, you'll be of no use at all," he hissed.

The Keeper, ever the voice of reason, stepped forward. "Malachi, your reign of darkness is over. Eldoria will resist, as will we."

Malachi laughed, the sound echoing eerily. "You think this is the end? I have only just begun."

Suddenly, the ground trembled, and a massive portal opened, drawing everything into its vortex. The monsters, the heroes, Lila in her cage – all were sucked in.

The group found themselves in a different realm, one even more foreign and distorted than the altered Eldoria. It was as though they were between worlds, a place of liminality.

Around them, the atmosphere was thick with a mix of hope and despair, of memories both cherished and forgotten. In the distance, they could see fragments of other realms, like shattered pieces of a mosaic.

As they tried to get their bearings, they noticed Lila's cage suspended in mid-air. She looked drained, the battle with Malachi taking its toll.

Elara approached the cage, trying to find a way to free her friend. "Lila, hold on," she said, determination evident in her voice.

Lila smiled weakly. "I'm glad you're here, Elara. I remember... everything."

From the shadows, Malachi emerged, his form even more menacing in this realm. "This is the Nexus," he declared, "the heart of all realms. And here, my power is absolute."

Kai, undeterred, charged at Malachi, but with a mere gesture, the sorcerer froze him in place.

Zara, her voice filled with anger, shouted, "Release him, Malachi!"

But the sorcerer only grinned. "You have no power here. I control the Nexus."

The Keeper, gazing at the fragmented realms, spoke up. "If you control the Nexus, then you control all of reality. This isn't just about Eldoria anymore."

Malachi nodded, a wicked smile playing on his lips. "Astute, Keeper. Once I merge these fragments, I will control every realm, every reality."

Elara, her spirit undaunted, declared, "We won't let you. We'll stop you, just like we always have."

But before she could act, Malachi began chanting, the fragments starting to merge. The group could feel the fabric of reality itself tearing, reshaping.

As the worlds began to blend, a powerful force surged through the Nexus. It was Lila, her cage amplifying her powers. "No, Malachi," she screamed. "I won't let you!"

In a blinding flash of light, the Nexus began to stabilize. But when the light faded, Lila was nowhere to be seen. In her place stood a portal, beckoning them.

Was Lila truly gone? What did the portal lead to? With heavy hearts, the group prepared to step through, unsure of what awaited them on the other side.

Chapter 24: Fragments and Friendships

The portal beckoned them like an oasis in a desert, its shimmering surface inviting yet mysterious. Elara, always the bravest of the bunch, was the first to step through, the swirling colors enveloping her. The Keeper followed closely, his vast knowledge guiding him. Zara, her hand clutching her blade, and the frozen form of Kai, carefully levitated by The Keeper's magic, entered next.

As they emerged on the other side, the environment was vastly different from the chaotic Nexus. They found themselves on a quiet street lined with quaint houses, not unlike their own childhood homes in Eldoria. Children played outside, their laughter echoing, reminding Elara of simpler times.

"Where are we?" Zara whispered, her voice barely audible amidst the innocent merriment.

The Keeper, his eyes scanning the surroundings, replied, "I believe we are within one of the fragmented realms, a shard of someone's memory."

They noticed that while everything seemed ordinary, there was a peculiar quality to the light and the colors, as though everything was seen through a soft, golden filter.

Elara, her thoughts still with Lila, murmured, "It's beautiful, yet haunting. Like a dream you can't wake up from."

As they ventured further, they stumbled upon a familiar sight. A schoolyard, children chasing after one another, and in the middle of it all stood a younger version of Lila, her hair flowing, her laughter infectious.

Elara's heart ached. "It's her memory," she whispered, tears forming. "We're inside Lila's happiest moment."

The younger Lila, seemingly sensing their presence, approached them. Her eyes, filled with innocence, looked at them curiously. "Who are you?" she asked, tilting her head.

Zara knelt, her warrior demeanor softening. "We are... friends, from a different time."

Young Lila's eyes sparkled. "Oh! I've always wanted friends from different times! Come, play with me!" And with that, she ran towards a swing set, beckoning them.

Despite the urgency of their mission, the group indulged in this fragment of joy. For that brief moment, there were no dark sorcerers or impending doom, just the pure, unadulterated joy of childhood.

As the sun began to set on this fragment, a sense of melancholy settled. Young Lila, her face glowing in the twilight, approached Elara. "You seem sad. Why?"

Elara, her voice choked with emotion, replied, "We miss our Lila. The one we know."

Young Lila, wisdom shining in her eyes, said, "Memories are powerful. They shape us, guide us. You're here for a reason. Remember that."

Suddenly, the world around them began to shake, the idyllic scene crumbling. The Keeper, alarmed, declared, "The fragment is collapsing! We need to move on!"

But just as they were about to retreat, they heard a voice, one they had been desperately hoping to hear.

"You found me."

Turning around, they saw Lila, not the young version from the memory but their Lila, her form translucent, hovering between realms.

"Lila!" Elara exclaimed, rushing forward, though she couldn't touch her friend. "Are you okay?"

Lila smiled, her voice echoing, "I am... in between. But I've seen the truth, Elara. Malachi's plan, it's bigger than we thought."

The Keeper, his face grave, asked, "What did you see?"

Lila's form flickered, "He doesn't just want to control the Nexus. He wants to rewrite history, shape reality to his own desires. He..."

But before she could continue, another tremor rocked the fragment, stronger than before.

"We're running out of time!" Zara shouted, clutching the paralyzed Kai.

Elara, desperation evident, said, "Lila, we'll find a way to bring you back, I promise."

Lila, her form growing fainter, replied, "Remember, Elara, memories shape us. Use them." And with that, she faded away.

As the fragment crumbled around them, another portal appeared. With no time to think, the group plunged in, hoping to find answers on the other side.

As they emerged, they found themselves in another fragment, this one dark, foreboding. Towering above them was a castle, its silhouette menacing against a blood-red sky. And standing at the entrance, his form more terrifying than they remembered, was Malachi.

"Welcome," he sneered, "to my memory."

The group, taken aback, braced themselves for the confrontation ahead, knowing the key to saving Lila and all of reality lay within Malachi's twisted past.

Chapter 25: Echoes of the Past

The sight of the towering castle, with its impenetrable stone walls and darkened windows, sent a shiver down Elara's spine. Malachi's presence, while foreboding, was a testament to the importance of the memory they had stepped into.

Malachi's smirk, ever so unsettling, never left his face. "Ah, visitors," he mused, his voice dripping with disdain. "Or perhaps intruders would be a more apt description."

The Keeper, his eyes narrowing, responded, "We are here for answers, Malachi. Your vendetta against the realms, the fragments, and Lila — it all ties back to your history. Show it to us."

Malachi laughed, a sound that echoed eerily through the barren landscape. "Very well," he conceded, "but remember, you asked for it."

The surroundings began to shift, the once imposing castle transforming into a more modest home, the air filled with the sounds of a bustling village.

A young Malachi, no more than a boy, was playing in the yard, his laughter innocent and free of malice. Zara, her warrior instincts ever-present, whispered to the group, "This doesn't seem like the setting of a dark sorcerer's origin."

But as they observed, the laughter was short-lived. Young Malachi's face turned to shock as he witnessed his home set ablaze, his parents trapped inside. A group of villagers, fear evident in their eyes, pointed at the boy, shouts of "witchcraft" and "curse" filling the air.

Malachi's voice, tinged with pain, echoed around them. "You wanted to see, didn't you? This is where it all began."

Elara, her heart heavy, approached the boy, her hand outstretched in comfort. But her hand passed through him, a mere memory unable to be consoled.

The scene shifted again. This time, they were in a dimly lit room. Books and scrolls were scattered everywhere, and young Malachi, now a teenager, was engrossed in a tome, his fingers tracing intricate symbols. Another figure, an old man with a long beard and piercing eyes, watched him intently.

"Master Eron," whispered The Keeper, recognizing the figure. "He was rumored to be the most powerful mage of his time."

The scene played out, young Malachi's thirst for knowledge and power evident. Master Eron, sensing the darkness growing in his pupil, tried to steer him towards the path of righteousness, but the seeds of vengeance had taken root.

A confrontation between master and student ensued, magical energies clashing, the room shaking from the intensity. But young Malachi, fueled by anger and pain, overpowered the old mage.

"I tried to guide him," said a translucent Master Eron, appearing beside The Keeper. "But his heart was consumed by darkness."

As the memory continued, the group watched Malachi's descent into darkness, his hunger for power growing, leading him to the Nexus and the fragmented realms.

Back in the present, or what felt like it, Malachi's sneer was back. "Now you see. Every action, every choice led me here. And you," he pointed at Elara, "cannot stop me."

Elara, her resolve strengthened, responded, "Your past may be filled with pain, Malachi, but it doesn't justify the hurt you've inflicted on others. We will stop you."

Suddenly, the world around them started to warp, the memory destabilizing. "What's happening?" shouted Zara, struggling to keep her footing.

Malachi, his expression one of genuine surprise, exclaimed, "It's not me! Something is pulling us out!"

The force was too strong, and the group found themselves being ejected from the memory, the scene blurring into a vortex of colors and sounds.

When the disorientation subsided, they were back in the Nexus, but not alone. Surrounding them were fragments of other memories, each a piece of Malachi's past. And in the distance, a silhouette, one that made Elara's heart race.

"Lila?" she called out.

The silhouette started to move closer, the features becoming clearer. But it wasn't Lila. It was someone else, someone they hadn't seen before, yet eerily familiar.

"Who are you?" demanded The Keeper, his staff at the ready.

The figure, a woman with flowing silver hair and piercing blue eyes, responded, "I am the Guardian of the Nexus. And you have all trespassed in a place you do not belong."

The group exchanged uneasy glances. They had faced Malachi's memories and the dark sorcerer himself, but this new entity exuded power on another level entirely.

"We seek to save our friend, Lila, and all the fragmented realms," Elara explained, hoping to find an ally.

The Guardian studied them, her gaze unwavering. "Your intentions may be noble, but the Nexus is not a playground. By entering Malachi's memories, you've endangered all of reality."

As the weight of their actions began to sink in, the Guardian's voice softened, "However, all is not lost. There is a way to set things right."

The group, hope renewed, listened intently.

"You must seek the Core of the Nexus," she began. "But be warned, it's a journey that few have

undertaken and even fewer have survived."

Before they could ask further questions, the Nexus started to shake violently.

"What's happening?" shouted Zara.

The Guardian, her face grave, replied, "Malachi, he's trying to break free. You must hurry."

As the tremors intensified, Elara's eyes met those of the Guardian, a silent understanding passing between them.

"We'll find the Core," she vowed.

But before they could move, a massive tear appeared in the Nexus, and through it, an army of dark creatures started pouring in, led by none other than Malachi.

Chapter 26: The Core's Secrets

The cavernous space of the Nexus echoed with the sounds of battle. Dark creatures, birthed from Malachi's twisted memories and intentions, lunged at Elara and her companions. Their forms were unsettling – half-remembered nightmares and fears from Malachi's past.

Zara, ever the warrior, drew her blade, the gleaming metal contrasting starkly against the ethereal backdrop of the Nexus. "We have to push through!" she yelled, slashing at the nearest creature.

Elara nodded, her own powers flaring to life, sending brilliant arcs of light towards their assailants. "We need to find the Core!"

The Keeper, staff in hand, chanted incantations that held back the advancing horde. "The Guardian mentioned it, but where could it be?"

Suddenly, a voice, melodic and calming, echoed around them. "Seek the place where memories are strongest."

It was the Guardian's voice, guiding them even in the midst of chaos.

Elara's eyes darted around, searching for a clue. "Where memories are strongest..." she murmured. "Of course! The first memory! Where it all began for Malachi."

The realization gave them direction, and with renewed vigor, they pressed forward, battling their way through the sea of creatures.

After what felt like hours, they reached the heart of the Nexus. Here, the memories swirled more densely, and at the center stood a magnificent crystal, pulsating with energy. The Core.

Elara approached it cautiously, her hand outstretched. The moment her fingers made contact, a rush of memories flooded her senses — not just Malachi's, but those of countless others who had traversed the realms.

"The Core... it's incredible," she whispered.

Zara, ever the protective friend, cautioned, "Be careful, Elara. We don't know its power."

But Elara's attention was elsewhere. She had spotted a memory — her memory — with Lila. They were children, playing in a sunlit meadow. The warmth of the sun, the scent of the flowers, the sound of Lila's laughter, it was all there.

Tears filled Elara's eyes. "Lila... I miss you," she whispered.

Suddenly, the Core's light intensified, and a portal opened before them. Through it, they could see a vast, uncharted realm, its beauty unmatched by any they had seen before.

The Keeper, his voice filled with awe, said, "It's the Origin Realm. The birthplace of all realities."

Malachi's voice, filled with rage, interrupted their wonder. "You think you've won, but this is far from over."

Turning, they saw Malachi, his form more formidable than before, power radiating from him. He was drawing energy from the Nexus itself.

"We have to stop him," Zara declared, her blade at the ready.

The ensuing battle was fierce. Malachi's newfound power gave him an edge, but Elara and her friends were not to be underestimated. With every blow, every spell, they pushed him back.

But as they fought, the Nexus began to destabilize, the memories becoming more chaotic, colliding with one another.

"We can't keep this up," The Keeper warned. "If the Nexus collapses, all realities will be lost."

Elara, her resolve unwavering, faced Malachi. "We have to end this, once and for all."

With a scream of pure determination, she channeled all her energy into a single, devastating blast, targeting the dark sorcerer.

The impact was immense. A shockwave rippled through the Nexus, throwing everyone off their feet. When the dust settled, Malachi was gone.

But their victory was short-lived. The Nexus was coming apart at the seams.

"We need to stabilize it!" The Keeper shouted.

"But how?" Zara asked, panic evident in her voice.

Elara, her gaze fixed on the Core, had an idea. "The Origin Realm! If we can link the Nexus to its source, maybe we can save it!"

Without hesitation, she plunged into the portal, her friends close behind.

The beauty of the Origin Realm was breathtaking. Lush meadows, sparkling rivers, and ancient forests stretched as far as the eye could see. But there was no time to admire the view.

Elara, drawing upon the realm's inherent magic, began weaving a spell. The others joined in, their combined energies forming a link between the Nexus and the Origin Realm.

Slowly, the Nexus began to stabilize. The memories settled, and a sense of calm returned.

Exhausted, the group collapsed on the grass, relief washing over them.

"We did it," Zara whispered.

The Keeper, a smile on his face, nodded. "Indeed. The Nexus is safe, and the realms are once again in balance."

Elara's thoughts, however, were on Lila. "We still have to find her."

Suddenly, a familiar voice echoed around them. "You've come so far, faced so many challenges. But your journey is far from over."

The group looked up to see the Guardian, her form shimmering in the light of the Origin Realm.

"Guardian," Elara began, "we need to find Lila. Can you help us?"

The Guardian, her gaze penetrating, replied, "Lila is not here. But she is not lost. Seek her in the

place where memories and dreams converge."

Before they could ask more, she vanished, leaving them with more questions than answers.

"What does she mean?" Zara asked, frustration evident in her voice.

The Keeper, deep in thought, replied, "I'm not sure. But we'll find out."

Elara, determination burning in her eyes, nodded. "We won't stop until we find Lila."

Little did they know, their biggest challenge was yet to come.

Chapter 27: The Place Between Dreams

The Origin Realm's vast expanse shimmered with a soft, welcoming light. Lush meadows spread in every direction, the grass swaying in a rhythmic dance. Here, the very essence of creation pulsed, echoing with a life force that felt almost familiar.

Elara, Zara, and the Keeper walked side by side, their mission clear, yet the path to finding Lila was shrouded in mystery. The Guardian's words echoed in Elara's mind: "Seek her in the place where memories and dreams converge."

"What did she mean, Keeper?" Zara asked, her frustration palpable.

The Keeper, usually so full of wisdom, looked thoughtful. "Dreams and memories are more interconnected than we often realize. Perhaps there's a place in this realm where they overlap, a sort of in-between."

Elara's heart ached with the weight of her mission. She had to find Lila, and the thought of wandering this vast realm indefinitely was daunting. "If only we had a guide," she murmured.

As if in response, a soft, melodious sound wafted through the air. It was neither a song nor a hum but something in between. The trio followed the sound, and it led them to a serene lake. The water was clear, reflecting the sky so perfectly that it was hard to tell where one ended and the other began.

By the lake stood a figure, her form shimmering like the morning dew. It was a dreamweaver, a being said to exist only in legends.

She spoke, her voice a soft whisper, "Seekers of the lost, you tread a path few dare to walk."

Elara stepped forward. "We're looking for Lila. Can you help us?"

The dreamweaver's gaze was penetrating, almost as if she could see the very depths of Elara's soul. "To find the lost, one must first lose oneself."

Zara, ever the pragmatic one, frowned. "I'm not sure riddles will help us now."

The dreamweaver smiled gently. "It's not a riddle, dear warrior. The place you seek is the Dreaming Glade. There, the memories of the past and the dreams of the future merge. But to enter, one must surrender to the dreamscape completely."

The Keeper nodded in understanding. "We must dream. Truly dream, letting go of our conscious selves."

Elara felt a mixture of excitement and fear. "How do we do that?"

The dreamweaver gestured to the lake. "The water here possesses the power to induce a dreamlike state. But remember, in the dreamscape, your deepest desires and fears will manifest. You must navigate through them to reach the Glade."

One by one, they approached the lake. With a deep breath, Elara touched the water. Instantly, a rush of images and emotions overwhelmed her.

She found herself in a familiar place - her childhood home. She was young again, playing with Lila in their secret hideout. The sun was shining, laughter filled the air, and for a moment, everything felt perfect.

But then the sky darkened. A storm approached, and Lila was being pulled away by an unseen force. Elara reached out, trying to grab her, but Lila was gone.

"No!" Elara cried out, tears streaming down her face. But then a voice, soft and comforting, whispered in her ear.

"It's not real, Elara. Remember why you're here."

Taking a deep breath, Elara focused on her mission. The storm dissipated, and the landscape shifted. Now she stood at the entrance of a beautiful glade. Trees with silver leaves surrounded a crystal-clear pool, and in the middle of the pool stood a platform.

On the platform was Lila.

Elara rushed forward, but a barrier stopped her. Lila looked at her, her eyes filled with sadness. "Elara, you have to make a choice."

A choice? Elara was confused. "What do you mean?"

Lila's voice was soft. "To save me, you have to let go. Truly let go."

Elara's heart ached. "I can't lose you again."

Lila smiled gently. "You won't. But sometimes, to find what we're looking for, we have to let go of the past."

Understanding dawned on Elara. She had been holding onto her memories of Lila, both good and bad. To save her, she had to embrace the present.

Closing her eyes, Elara took a deep breath. She let go of her fears, her regrets, and her memories. She focused on the here and now, on her love for Lila and her determination to save her.

The barrier vanished. Elara stepped onto the platform and hugged Lila tightly. "I found you."

Lila hugged her back. "And I was never truly lost."

The dreamscape began to fade, and Elara found herself back by the lake, Lila by her side. Zara and the Keeper were there too, looking relieved.

"We did it," Zara said, smiling.

The Keeper nodded. "The balance has been restored."

Elara looked at Lila, tears in her eyes. "I thought I'd lost you."

Lila smiled. "You'll never lose me. Not truly."

The dreamweaver approached, her form shimmering in the soft light. "You have done well, seekers. The realms are in balance once more."

Elara nodded. "Thank you for your guidance."

The dreamweaver smiled. "Remember, the true journey is not in seeking new landscapes but in having new eyes. Cherish the memories but live in the present."

With that, she vanished, leaving the group in the serene beauty of the Origin Realm.

The journey had been long and challenging, but they had found what they were looking for. Not just Lila but a deeper understanding of themselves and the interconnectedness of all things.

As they made their way back to their own realm, Elara felt a profound sense of peace. The adventure was over, but a new chapter in their lives was just beginning.

The End